TRAUMA

Psychiatrist Charlie Weir has tackled every kind of trauma during his years in New York City, but he's yet to resolve the conflicts within his own family, not least the bitter rivalry with his brother Walt. And he's never overcome the terrible blunder that lost him his wife and daughter . . . When Walt introduces him to the beautiful Nora Chiara, they quickly fall for each other. But soon, her vulnerability, which first attracted him, begins to sour their relationship. And as he probes at the source of her distress, something deep in his own unconscious mind arouses a horrifying suspicion . . .

PATRICK McGRATH

◆

TRAUMA

Complete and Unabridged

ULVERSCROFT
Leicester

First published in Great Britain in 2008 by
Bloomsbury Publishing Plc
London

First Large Print Edition
published 2009
by arrangement with
Bloomsbury Publishing Plc
London

British Library CIP Data

McGrath , Patrick, *1950 –*
Trauma
1. Psychiatrists- -New York (State)- -New York- -Fiction.
2. Psychological fiction. 3. Large type books.
I. Title
823.9'14–dc22

ISBN 978–1–84782–820–0

Published by
F. A. Thorpe (Publishing)
Anstey, Leicestershire

Set by Words & Graphics Ltd.
Anstey, Leicestershire
Printed and bound in Great Britain by
T. J. International Ltd., Padstow, Cornwall

This book is printed on acid-free paper

For Maria

1

My mother's first depressive illness occurred
when I was seven years old, and I felt it was
my fault. I felt I should have prevented it.
This was about a year before my father left
us. His name was Fred Weir. In those days he
could be generous, amusing, an expansive
man — my brother, Walt, plays the role at
times — but there were signs, perceptible to
me if not to others, when an explosion was
imminent. Then the sudden loss of temper,
the storming from the room, the slamming
door at the end of the hall and the appalled
silence afterward. But I could deflect all this.
I would play the fool, or be the baby, distract
him from the mounting wave of boredom and
frustration he must have felt at being trapped
within the suffocating domestic atmosphere
my mother liked to foster. Later, when she
began writing books, she fostered no
atmosphere at all other than genteel squalor
and heavy drinking and gloom. But by then
my father was long gone.

In those days we lived in shabby discomfort
in a large apartment on West Eighty-seventh
Street, where my brother lives with his family

today. I never contested Walt's right to have it after Mom died, and have come to terms with the fact that to me she left nothing. Indeed, it amuses me that she would throw this one last insult in my face from beyond the grave. It was more appropriate that Walt should have the apartment, given the size of his family, and me living alone, although Walt didn't actually need the apartment. Walt was a wealthy man — Walter Weir, the painter? But I don't resent this, although having said that, or rather, had I heard one of my patients say it, I would at once detect the anger behind the words. With consummate skill I would then extricate the truth, bring it up to the surface where we both could face it square: *You hated your mother! You hate her still!*

I am, as will be apparent by now, a psychiatrist. I do professionally that which you do naturally for those you care for, those whose welfare has been entrusted to you. My office was for many years on Park Avenue, which is less impressive than it sounds. The rent was low, and so were my fees. I worked mostly with victims of trauma, who of all the mentally disturbed people in the city of New York feel it most acutely, that they are owed for what they've suffered. It makes them slow to pay their bills. I chose this line of work because of my mother, and I am not alone in

2

this. It is the mothers who propel most of us into psychiatry, usually because we have failed them.

Often a patient will be referred to me, and after the preliminaries have been completed and he, or more usually she, is settled comfortably, this will be her question: Where would you like me to begin?

'Just tell me what you've been thinking about.'

'Nothing.'

'What were you thinking about on your way to this appointment?'

And so it begins. I listen. Mine is a profession that might on the surface appear to suit the passive personality. But don't be too quick to assume that we are uninterested in power. I sit there pondering while you tell me your thoughts, and with my grunts and sighs, my occasional interruptions, I guide you toward what I believe to be the true core and substance of your problem. It is not a scientific endeavor. No, I feel my way into your experience with an intuition based on little more than a few years of practice, and reading, and focused introspection; in other words, there is much of art in what I do.

My mother did eventually recover, but there is a strong correlation between depression and anger and at some level she stayed angry. It was largely directed at my father, of course. I have a clear memory of the day I first became aware of my parents' dynamic of abandonment and rage. Fred had taken Walter and me to lunch, a thing he did occasionally when he was in town and remembered that he had two sons living on West Eighty-seventh Street. For me these were stressful events, starting with the cab ride to an East Side steakhouse, though in fact any time spent with my father was stressful. One summer he took us on a road trip upstate to a hotel in the Catskills, a journey of pure unmitigated hell, the endless hours sitting beside Walter in the back of the Buick as we drove through the endless mountains, and the atmosphere never less than explosive —

Fred Weir was still handsome then, his dark hair swept back from a sharp peak in a high-templed forehead, a tall, athletic fellow with a charming grin. He wasn't a successful man but he gave the impression of being one, and when he took us out to lunch I marveled at the peremptory tone with which he addressed the waiters, brisk unsmiling men in starched white aprons who, in that adult room of wood paneling and cigar smoke, thoroughly intimidated the lanky, nervous adolescent I then was. My anxiety was not eased by the presence of steak knives with heavy wooden handles and sharp serrated blades, and a sort of diabolical trolley that was wheeled, steaming, to the table by a stout man with a pencil mustache who with the flourish of a gleaming knife indicated the meat and demanded to know where I wanted it carved.

When Fred grew bored with us and showed signs of calling for the check, Walt would ask him for investment advice, claiming to have considerable funds stashed away. Walt was always more curious about our father than I was. As a boy he was intrigued as to what went on in our parents' bedroom, when they shared a bedroom, that is. He wanted to get in there and find out what they *did*.

Mom was distressed when we returned from these outings, having in our absence awoken to the possibility that Fred might exert a stronger influence over her boys than she did and that we too would then be lost to her. It fell to me to assure her of our love and loyalty. Then she lavished her affection on me for a while, until she grew distracted and drifted off down the hall to her study. Hearing the door close and the *tap-tap-tap* of the typewriter, I knew she would not come out before it was time for a cocktail. I was comforted by the sound of the typewriter. If she was typing then she wasn't crying, although later she was able to do both at once.

But I remember one day when we returned to the apartment and she wasn't waiting in the hallway as we came up the stairs. This was unusual. We let ourselves in and at once heard her crying in her bedroom. It was pitiful. Walter said he was going out again, I could do what I wanted. I see myself with great clarity at that moment. The choice was simple. I could walk out of the apartment with him and spend an hour or two in Central Park, or I could go and knock on my mother's bedroom door and ask her what was wrong. I remember sitting down on the chair in the hallway, beside the low desk with the telephone on it, where she always left her keys on the tray and fixed her hair in the mirror on the wall above it.

'I'm not waiting,' Walt said from the front door.

A sudden fresh gust of misery from the bedroom.

'I think I'll stay.'

'Suit yourself,' he said, and the front door closed behind him.

For another minute I sat on the chair in the hallway, then stood up and walked slowly toward her room. This is how psychiatrists are made.

⋆   ⋆   ⋆

Much of my later childhood and adolescence followed this pattern. I did not make friends easily, and I was more content by far with a book than with the company of my contemporaries. Walter by contrast was a gregarious boy and often brought his friends back to the apartment. This was a source of pleasure to my mother, although if she was depressed she would withdraw to her bedroom. At times like this it was a cause of concern to me that Walter's friends made so much noise. I remember I stood in the doorway of the living room once and asked them to be quiet, as Mom was resting. They were dancing to Bill Haley. Walter would have been about seventeen; I was three years younger. I remember he turned the record player off and they all stared at me, six or seven of them, older kids I'd seen in the corridors of the high school we attended on the Upper West Side.

'What did you say?' said Walter.

If it hadn't been for the fact that Mom was trying to sleep I would have fled.

'I said, I think you should turn it down.'

They all stared at me in silence. It was a form of mockery. 'What did you say?' said Walter again.

'Turn it down! She's trying to get some sleep!'

He looked at the others and solemnly repeated my words. They started laughing. They slapped their thighs, they yelped like hyenas; they lifted their heads and howled, all to humiliate me. Then Mom's bedroom door opened down the hall. She shuffled toward the living room, yawning. She was in her robe, barefoot, and she hadn't brushed her hair. It was the middle of the afternoon and I felt embarrassed for her in front of Walter's friends, who had fallen silent. She stood in the doorway and asked what was going on, and Walter told her. She was still half asleep. She turned to me.

'Don't be silly, Charlie, I was only reading. You people have fun, I don't care.'

She went back to her room with a wave of her hand and I left the apartment feeling like a fool.

★ ★ ★

When I returned to New York after my residency at Johns Hopkins, I didn't move back to Eighty-seventh Street. Mom told me she didn't want me in the apartment. She said she needed silence in order to write. I understood what she was telling me. It was not a rejection, though it was framed in those terms, because she also gave me a new set of keys. Don't abandon me, she was saying. She was stabilized on antidepressants but there were still times when she would suddenly, precipitately go down, and then it was me she needed.

One such occasion was when Fred remarried, to a woman many years younger, which Mom found hard to accept. For a long time I had known she still loved him, and despite her salty disdain — 'What a *rat*,' she'd spit — it escaped nobody who knew her well that she continued to carry a torch for this feckless man. In both the novels she published in those years she drew thinly veiled portraits of him, and the authorial attitude to these philandering crooks was one of ill-concealed affection. But his second marriage hit her hard and, as I'd feared, she suffered a rapid relapse. I went to the apartment as soon as I heard.

She was in her bedroom. All the drapes were closed even though it was the middle of the day. She lay on the bed with her back to the door, her legs pulled up. She was not fully clothed. She heard me come in but she didn't move.

'Mom?' I sat on the side of the bed. For some minutes there was silence in the room. There was a faint smell of stale perfume and cigarette smoke. 'How long have you been in here?'

No answer.

'Do you want me to run you a bath?'

I knew what I was saying. She reared up on one elbow and over her shoulder shot me a pathetic look. Her eyes were ringed with dark shadows: she was a haunted, frightened creature, almost unrecognizable to me.

Then she sank back once more. From her near-fetal position she murmured, 'I smell bad. You don't have to tell me.'

'You don't smell bad. I just thought you might like to get in the tub.'

Silence once more. Then up on the elbow again. 'That rat.'

'I know.'

'Have you seen him?'

'No.'

'You're lying.'

'Let me run you a bath.'

She didn't refuse. In my experience a depressive episode is not life-threatening when there is still concern for personal hygiene.

When I came back from the bathroom she was sitting humped on the side of the bed with her legs dangling down, inspecting her fingernails. She looked like an old bird in her oversize sweater and black tights, a sick old bird with a broken wing. 'Is she beautiful?'

'No.'

'How do you know?'

Quick as a viper, this — how did I know unless I'd met her? 'I just know,' I said.

'Cunt.'

I wasn't sure if she meant me, or my father, or his young bride. I didn't ask. When her bath was ready I told her I'd be in the living room. It was no better there in terms of stagnant air, brimming ashtrays, gloom and such. Torn photographs on the rug in front of the fireplace, a few charred embers in the grate. I pulled back the drapes, opened the windows, tidied the place as best I could. I went back to the bathroom and tapped on the door.

'You all right in there?'

'Fuck off.'

'Ma?'

'You met her. You traitor.'

It would almost be comic if this were somebody else's mother. If I weren't alert to the reality of her suffering. If she hadn't already given me so much cause for concern. How can any man see his mother in pain and not do everything in his power to relieve that pain?

11

★ ★ ★

When these episodes were becoming more frequent there would be periods of days or even weeks when I left my office in the evening and went straight up to Eighty-seventh Street. Often I stayed the night and slept in my old room. Walt refused to visit Mom when she was depressed, and I got angry with him about it. I remember him saying that Mom didn't want to see him, she only wanted to see me.

'Don't be absurd,' I said. 'It's you she adores.'

I remember having this argument in Walt's loft on Chambers Street. He didn't stop working. A big messy canvas was pinned to the wall, a field of red with thin black vertical spikes at irregular intervals. He was smoking a cigar.

'That's exactly why she doesn't want me coming around,' he said. 'She doesn't want me to see her like *that*.'

'Oh Walter, what new bullshit is this?'

Walt and I could get angry at each other in seconds. It alarmed others. It worried Agnes, my wife, to whom I was still married at the time, when she first saw it happen, that two otherwise civilized men could so quickly become so abusive.

12

'Think! Isn't that what you're meant to be good at? She doesn't want me around when she looks like death. She wants me when she's at her best!'

He noticed that he was dripping paint on the floor. He clamped the cigar between his teeth and plunged his brush into a jar of dirty water.

'So you get the good mother and I get the mad mother. Thanks a lot, Walt. Christ, you're a selfish man.'

'I didn't fucking set it up!'

I don't remember if I responded to this. I think I may have turned my head and with a sickly, injured expression stared out the window. The World Trade Center was under construction then, two massive, fretted frames of red girders poking into the sky. When I turned back Walt was absently wiping his fingers on a rag.

'Any message for her?' I said from the door.

Now he was at the sink with his back to me. When he didn't reply I repeated the question.

'No!'

Years later I remembered the argument and realized he was right. When she was in a state of abject despair she was indifferent to the impression she made on me, but Walt must be spared, Walt was excused. So he learned early on that he need never make an effort with Mom, and strangely her love thrived on his neglect. She seemed to think the fact that he so rarely visited her proved he was much too busy, certainly far busier than me, but of course he was so much more successful than me. She said this once to Agnes.

'But Charlie's a brilliant psychiatrist,' said Agnes.

Mom's reply was a classic of maternal spite.

'Oh, anyone can be a psychiatrist,' she said. 'It takes talent to be an artist.'

★   ★   ★

The call came from her housekeeper. It was early February 1979. She'd come in that morning and found her unconscious on the bedroom floor. By the time I reached the apartment her own doctor was there, arranging for her to be admitted to Beth Israel. He and I stood apart for a minute or two and spoke quietly about what would happen next. I was at her bedside in the hospital when she came to, and so was Walt. I remember how her hand lifted off the covers. It was like a little bird trying to take flight, and failing, but it was an ugly little bird,

14

clawed and liver-spotted.

'Mom?'

The eyes were bleary. She was confused. Her voice was weak. She wanted to talk about her family.

'No, Mom, just rest, you can tell us later.'

The light all at once flared in those watery eyes and she seized my wrist. She tried to sit up but couldn't. Nor could she talk anymore. A little later she fell asleep and we left her. When we were out in the corridor the elevator opened and my father emerged. I told him she needed to rest. Walt suggested we go somewhere for a drink.

We sat at a quiet table in a hotel bar a couple of blocks from the hospital. The years had not been kind to Fred Weir and his decay was marked. He'd failed to shave properly, leaving patches of stubble on his throat and jaw. His suit was cheap, the cuffs frayed, and the collar of the shirt was yellowed. More telling was the faint air of apology that clung to him now and, too, the dampness, the lifelessness in the eyes, all of which suggested heavy drinking, loss of vitality, collapse of self-esteem. Also, he'd done jail time in Florida for a firearms offense. He looked like what he was, I thought: a loser. As a boy I always tried to please this man, to keep him from hurting my mother, and what a waste.

15

He wasn't worth it, and I believed at one time that this was why she gave all her love to Walter, and none to me. Physically, and to an extent temperamentally, I resembled Fred Weir, and the older I got the clearer it became. With his long, pallid face, his shambling gait, the lick of gray, greasy hair falling over his forehead, the ingratiating grin that would once have opened doors, opened hearts — he was the template, I was the issue.

Walt by contrast was built on Hallam lines, Mom's family, big in the chest and across the shoulders, florid, shaggy, a barrel of a man, a locomotive, where I was a stork, a palm. Fred was a washout. A soak. 'What are you drinking, Dad?' said Walt.

It was a small, gloomy room with a padded bar, a few round tables with lamps, the lingering odor of cigar smoke. Some sort of Muzak was playing. We were the only ones in there besides the sad-faced man in a short white jacket who stood behind the bar. Walt half-turned in his chair to bring him over. Fred settled his elbows on the table and pulled out a pack of cigarettes, and a certain ease was at once apparent. He was at home in a bar. 'I think in the circumstances a dry martini, Walter.'

'I don't want anything,' I said.

'Two dry martinis,' he said.

16

'Olives or a twist?'

'Twist.'

The three of us sat in silence until the drinks arrived.

'So Charlie, what's the story?' Walt said at last.

'A vascular accident. That's a stroke. There could be another in the next twenty-four to forty-eight hours.'

'Which means what?'

'It'll probably kill her.'

'Oh god,' Fred said.

'That troubles you?' I said.

'Back off, Charlie,' said Walt.

I knew why I was so angry, and that it wasn't my father's fault, but I saw no particular reason not to displace it onto him, and if I could make Walt mad at the same time then so much the better. Walt watched me over the rim of the glass as he took a sip of his martini. Fred left his untouched, as though to indicate his indifference to alcohol. I wished I didn't see this; I wished the three of us could just have a drink without rancor, like regular guys.

'So, Walter,' Fred said, 'I read about you in the paper.'

'Where do you live now, Dad?'

'I travel a lot,' he said. 'There's an office in Jersey City that can usually find me.'

17

The tone was distinctly evasive.

'So what do you do, Fred?' I said. 'What does all this traveling involve?'

'It wouldn't interest you, Charlie.'

'Sure it would.'

'Lay off,' said Walt.

'You two boys going to have a fight?' said Fred, picking up his drink at last. He'd always encouraged our fights when we were boys. He liked to see us going at it.

Again we sat in silence. Fred finished his martini and Walt signaled for another round. Fred stared at the table with his hands laid flat on either side of his glass, a cigarette between his fingers. He looked up. The gray skin of his jowls and cheeks had acquired a few purple spots of bloom.

'You think it cost me nothing to leave your mother?' he said.

'No,' Walt said.

'Yes,' I said.

Fred leaned over and gripped my arm, shaking his head. He looked as though he was about to cry.

'Christ, man, you're a fucking *shrink*,' said Walt.

'I hate that word,' I said.

Fred sat with his elbows on the table, his mouth pressed to his clasped fingers, the cigarette smoke drifting across his troubled, sagging, blotchy face.

'That's what you really think, son?' he said.

I sat regarding my father and nodded my head.

'Shit, Charlie,' Walt said.

I stood up and without looking at either one of them I walked out of the hotel and hailed a cab. I wanted to be at home listening to classical music with my eyes closed. I wanted my mother not to die.

★   ★   ★

But die she did. It was as I said. The next stroke came within forty-eight hours. I'd spent many of those hours at her bedside. She reverted again to the subject of her family. She said she had misled me, that she'd given me to believe they came to America much earlier than they had. It seemed to matter that I understand this.

'What sort of people were they, Mom?' I said.

She was doped, bleary, weak. Her fingers trembled on my wrist. Her face grew light, almost humorous, like a child's. Or like a young woman's face, the young woman she once had been.

'Actors, Charlie! They were actors!'

It was our last conversation. The funeral

took place at a Presbyterian church on the corner of Eighty-sixth and Amsterdam that she'd never set foot in. There was a death notice in the *Times*, and perhaps fifty people showed up. They were invited back to the apartment afterward while Fred and Walt and I accompanied the coffin to a cemetery in the Bronx. The atmosphere in the car was strained. It was a Lincoln town car and my father elected to sit up front with the driver. He and I were wearing black suits but Walt sported a dark blue affair with broad lapels and one of those absurd ties, huge and floppy, deep purple in color. It was the fashion then. His side-burns made him look like a werewolf. I believe that of the three of us he was the least affected by our mother's death. He was gazing out the window as we drove north, and I could tell his thoughts were elsewhere. I leaned forward and gripped my father's shoulder.

'Is that you, Charles?' he said, turning his head so I had his face in profile.

'You all right, Dad?'

'Sure. What about you?'

I gave the shoulder a squeeze and withdrew my hand. It did not go unremarked by the psychiatrist inside my skull that by any standards this was pretty rudimentary com-munication; but it was all I was capable of, with him.

When we returned to the apartment Agnes was there. Since the separation I'd seen her only when I went down to Fulton Street to pick up our daughter, Cassie. Agnes had barely spoken to me in years.

'Hello, Charlie,' she said.

'Hello, Agnes.'

'I'm so sorry.'

'I know. Thanks.'

We embraced. I held her close. Over her shoulder I could see Cassie, aged eight, gazing at me. Behind her, stony-faced, stood her stepfather, Leon. On the rare occasions over the years when the three of us, Agnes, Cassie and I, had been together, and by an act of willful erasure I succeeded in forgetting the fissure I had created and glimpsed instead a family, it aroused in me a strong gush of pleasure. It was the idea of the three of us under one roof, living unexceptional routines and bound to one another by ties of unthinking affection. Such ordinariness struck me as the very acme of human achievement.

Then other people were crowding in, old family friends, my mother's few intimates, women like herself if such a thing can be imagined, also the people she'd met in her late-blooming career as a novelist.

Later, when they had all left, I sat alone with the empty glasses and dirty plates and ashtrays while the housekeeper cleaned up, and felt an alarming plummeting sensation in my body. It was accompanied by what I can only call a wave of the purest blackness. I recognized it as the sort of precipitate mental collapse that had characterized my mother's depressions, and I felt, too, as I watched myself falling like a stone down a well, that I'd become infected with her illness. I saw it then, Mom's depression, as a parasite deprived of its host and finding me instead. A perverse idea, but I understood why my mood had changed so dramatically. In a compressed few hours I had encountered every person with whom I'd ever known intimacy save one, that being my mother, and she was dead. I was estranged from all of them except one, that being my daughter, who lived not with me but with her mother. I was approaching forty and I no longer regarded my life as possessing unlimited potential, or any at all. I felt my own isolation strongly, and while I was still sexually active the possibility of proper human intimacy seemed every day to recede further from me.

I sat by the window in my mother's living room as the housekeeper ferried stacks of dishes and trays of glasses to the kitchen. Outside, the light faded as the long winter afternoon came to an end. I could hear the woman working in the kitchen and for a second imagined it was Mom in there. After a while she came back into the living room and turned the lights on. She cried out when she saw me, as though she'd seen a ghost.

'Are you still here, Doctor?'

I got up out of my chair and left the apartment. Descending the staircase I remembered a story about a man in an asylum. This man believes that his psychiatrist, whom he has met only once, is busy working on his case, finding the solution to his problem. It keeps him going. Then, after some months, he sees him again. The psychiatrist pats him on the back and asks what his name is, and what seems to be the problem. This was my mood. I felt as though I'd been putting my faith in some absent being who was working on my problem. When my mother died I realized that nobody was working on my problem, in fact no one even knew what my problem was.

2

The building on Eighty-seventh Street had a small foyer with a bronze pot for umbrellas, an old wing chair and a faded rug. It was always full of shadows, especially in the gloom of a dying day. As I came down the last flight of stairs a figure rose from the chair and moved toward me. She had waited for me. We stood there in our overcoats, facing each other, and then we embraced.

'Look at the state of you,' she murmured.

We took a cab in the rain to Twenty-third Street. Agnes had never been in the apartment before, and she moved around it as women do, as cats do, in new places, feeling for the spirit, I suppose. We had barely spoken in the cab. I was very deeply moved by this act of generosity, or affection, or whatever it sprang from; for some reason it made me think of the early days, when I was running the psych unit on the East Side and we stood shoulder to shoulder, Agnes and I, comrades as much as lovers. Now I felt that the bond had endured despite the years of anger, despite everything.

'You're going to miss her, Charlie.'

'Oh yes.'

Her being with me like this, keeping company with the bereaved — given that I had nobody else, this was a compassionate gesture, though what more it signified I couldn't say. Agnes remained physically attractive to me, and perhaps as a function of death's proximity I wanted very badly to hold her close to me then. But that was not for me to ask.

'All right, Charlie, come here.'

She was on the sofa. I switched off all the lights except for the lamp in the corner and sat down next to her. Turning toward me she took my face in her hands and, with some deliberation, kissed me. I became at once feverish and she permitted this, then she let herself be led into the bedroom where the fierceness of my desire surprised me but apparently not her, perhaps because she already understood sex as a kind of cathartic abreaction to the fact of death. I hadn't had sex with an emotional intimate since she and I had last been together, that was before Danny, her brother, died. But I hadn't been celibate in the meanwhile; there was a building at Thirty-third and Lex where in a large, fourth-floor apartment women sold sex every night of the week. One of the women I visited there resembled Agnes sufficiently

— the same lanky, small-breasted body, hair the same shade of pale straw — that I was able to sustain an identification. We did nothing particularly kinky. I was happy just to have her wrap her legs around me as Agnes used to, and do that same thing with her pelvis. The woman apparently had no feelings either way as to what name I moaned into her stiffly lacquered hair.

Later we lay comfortably in the darkness. Through the narrow space where the blind failed to reach the top of the window the lights of the city played across the ceiling. Agnes was mildly surprised to find herself in my bed, though not alarmed; there was no convulsion of panic or guilt. She hadn't planned this, she told me, but when she'd seen the depth of my grief back on Eighty-seventh Street, it was inconceivable to her that I should be left alone in such pain. I had once left *her* alone in pain, and I knew, because she'd told me, that she would never forget it.

★   ★   ★

We had met almost ten years earlier. I was running a psychiatric unit in an old city hospital then, and one of my responsibilities was to sit in with a group of vets. One night a young woman lingered in the doorway after the meeting ended. The vets had all dispersed, and I was writing up my notes. When I became aware of her I stood up and asked if I could help her, and she told me she was Danny Magill's sister. She said he didn't know she was there.

She was leaning against the door frame with her arms folded. I could see the resemblance, physically at least. She was about twenty-two, and like her brother she possessed a watchful kind of reserve. Bony physique, pale skin, dishwater blond hair with thick bangs covering her forehead and falling over her eyes. She seemed to be inspecting me. She was grinning, I remember, as though I amused her.

'You want to talk?'

'I don't know,' she said.

But she pushed herself off the door frame and sat down. She was wearing a short denim skirt and cowboy boots, and a black T-shirt with a skull and crossbones on it. I remember a lot of women like that in those days, tall, self-reliant women, skeptical and independent. Back then I was less cautious than I became later. A woman like this I wanted to get close to. She was my type. The gray eyes were direct, aggressively so, and I liked that. It was a humid summer night. The traffic on

27

First Avenue was heavy. An ambulance siren grew piercingly shrill, then suddenly fell silent.

'You think he's getting anything out of it?'

'He keeps showing up.'

I leaned against the table, watching her. She stood up and wandered around the room.

'Does he talk to you?'

'No,' I said.

'Me either.'

All at once she contracted her facial muscles as though to rid herself of an unwelcome thought. What was it? Her brother, of course. Danny. What did she want from me? Reassurance, some platitude regarding his eventual recovery. Back like he was before.

'We were close once. He won't talk to me at all now. What's your name?'

I told her. We stared at each other for a few seconds. There was a clarity, a frankness between us, and I felt I'd known her for years. I also felt she didn't want platitudes but something more substantial.

'I just don't get it,' she said.

'You just have to wait till he's ready.'

'Why?'

Why! Yes, she wanted to know. She wanted to hear me talk about him. I told her these men had been profoundly traumatized by what they'd been through.

'What does that mean?'

'A shock to the mind so intense you can't get rid of it. You can force it out of your consciousness but you never forget it. And it comes back.'

'How?'

'Nightmares. Flashbacks.'

She asked me more questions. I tried to answer them. I remember sitting forward on the edge of a chair, one hand on my knee and the other chopping at the air, giving emphasis, trying to make it all clear for her. Her posture mirrored mine. She too sat forward, listening intently, frowning, elbows on her knees. We were both tall and skinny, both long-haired, earnest, serious. From the start we were like a pair of twins.

'So we wait.'

'How long?'

I shrugged. 'Long as it takes.'

'Have you done a lot of this stuff?'

'We're making it up as we go along.'

Now she laughed, a short bark like a cork exploding from a bottle. She sat back, pushed her hand into her bag and pulled out rolling tobacco and papers. I was tired. I wanted to go home. I had to be on the ward first thing in the morning. But I didn't want to let her out of my sight.

'You know what they call you?' she said.

'What do they call me?'

'You don't know?'

She was fully alive to me now. We were fully alive to each other.

'No.'

'Captain Nightmare.'

'I knew that.'

She thought it was flattering. 'And Christ,' she said, 'those guys have nightmares. Don't they?'

'Oh, they have nightmares all right.'

'So what do I do, Captain Nightmare?'

'I think you just have to give him room,' I said.

She nodded, then lit her cigarette with a Zippo. It is an image I have always held on to, for some reason, how she sat with her fingers cupped around the cigarette, frowning, her hair falling forward, the flare of the Zippo and the tobacco catching. Outside, the low rumble of traffic, a muted car horn, a blast of music, the Doors. She snapped the lighter shut.

'I feel better.' She blew smoke at the ceiling.

'You're welcome.'

I locked up. She walked down the corridor beside me, her boots clanking on the floor.

The strip lighting cast a harsh glare on the green walls. A janitor slipped by and murmured good night. From somewhere high in the building we heard a man shouting.

Out on the sidewalk she threw away the cigarette. 'You want to go for a beer, Captain?'

Second Avenue on a hot summer night. Cabs, cop cars, long-hooded Cadillacs with their windows rolled down, a woman screaming, horns honking, the sidewalk crowded. We went to Smithy's, a seedy joint with its doors wide open to the street and rock music spilling out. We got our beers and found a corner and talked some more about her brother. They'd grown up in a town out on the island. Their father was a builder, also a drunk. She was a grad student at NYU in sociology. She'd won a scholarship. Later, after a couple of beers, on the steps of an apartment building, she stood with her back to the wall, hips canted forward and her hands behind her head, and let me kiss her. I covered her body as headlights raked the doorway. I kissed her again. Then she pushed herself off the wall and kissed me back, spreading her fingers across my cheeks. We stared at each other, very close now, in that clear-eyed, candid way we'd been looking at each other for the last hour. We were both panting slightly, and grinning like a pair of conspirators. We were in this together, whatever it was. Compadres. The mood suddenly broke.

'Okay, I'm headed uptown,' she said.

'I'm downtown.'

'So, thanks.'

She stuck out her arm and we shook hands. Hers was a thin, strong, bony hand. I crossed the street, then turned and watched her stride away, contained and imperturbable. Emphatically not one of my haunted women.

★　★　★

She turned toward me in the bed and propped her head on her chin to gaze at me where I lay staring at the shifting patterns of light on the ceiling. Somewhere on Tenth Avenue a garbage truck rumbled to life and moved off with a hiss and a clatter. A distant siren was audible to the east, a wail within the indistinct constant restless murmur of the city late at night.

'What will they say at home?'

'Nobody's at home. I'm a free woman tonight.'

'You knew, did you, that this would be the worst night?'

She nodded. She reached over to me,

stroked my cheek and ran her finger along my lips. 'Charlie,' she said.

'Will you come here again?'

'Maybe.'

I reached for her. I believed that this 'maybe' meant we might have some sort of private arrangement. But I feared that her tentative acquiescence could vanish as suddenly as it had materialized. For although Agnes was at that moment as open and tender toward me as she'd ever been, I doubted she would be the same woman in the morning. So I said nothing more. A little later we fell asleep, still tangled in each other's limbs.

★ ★ ★

Her brother was one of the worst damaged of the vets in the group, although I didn't tell her that the night we met. I'd just completed my residency at Johns Hopkins when I was offered the psych unit, and despite the squalid condition of the facilities and the evident demoralization of the staff, I'd accepted the job at once. I was young for such an appointment, but I was ambitious, I was qualified and I was deeply relieved to be back home after the years in Baltimore.

But New York had deteriorated in my

absence. I was horrified at the decay into which the city had sunk, and if the worst of it fell on the poor — garbage everywhere, streetlights broken, phone booths smashed up, crime out of control, people at each other's throats, on and on — that was nothing compared to what was happening to the mentally ill. It was too late for most of the pathetic creatures who shuffled up and down the wards, who for years had been so completely dependent on the institution that there was no possibility of their ever getting out again, though many had got out, had been thrown out, in fact, and were wandering the city in rags, babbling to themselves and living in filth, truly the wretched of the earth. At the end of my first day I sat exhausted in my office and asked myself what possible point there was in carrying on.

But I was young, and I refused to be disheartened: I *would* make a difference. With the support of my boss, a man named Sam Pike, I planned to turn the unit into a model of the sort of progressive mental-health treatment I'd been exposed to at Johns Hopkins. I suppose I was no different from tens of thousands of young Americans then, disgusted by not only the political establishment but all social institutions, orthodox psychiatry not least, and committed to the idea that without radical change our society was done for. Central to this movement, if that's what it was, was our opposition to the war. For this reason I was determined to do what I could for the men returning from Southeast Asia with severe psychological damage, what was once called combat fatigue, and before that shell shock.

I will not forget the stuffy, smoke-filled room where we met in the basement of the hospital; the room where I met Agnes. I remember a dozen or more vets sitting in a rough circle. I see them grinning as though for a group photo, each of those emotionally shattered but still defiant men in their T-shirts and blue jeans, their baseball caps, their tattoos, men in their twenties mostly who'd seen what no human being should ever have to see and the pain of it stamped on their faces like boot prints. They looked old beyond their years, sitting forward with elbows on knees, or with legs flung out, an arm over the back of the chair, eyes turned up to the ceiling and a cigarette always burning between their fingers. They startled easily and sought refuge in street drugs and alcohol, and their symptoms would later be tied to posttraumatic stress disorder — a term that didn't exist then. They'd seen their buddies die and wanted to know why it wasn't them.

They felt defiled. They felt, many of them, that they were already dead.

* * *

It was three weeks before she visited me again. I had not tried to contact her. I preferred to test my solitude to the limits of endurance, and those I had yet to reach. But the hours I'd spent with her the night of my mother's funeral had awoken in me what I could only think of as a hunger: Agnes was the only woman I had ever properly *loved*. I had often thought about what I meant by the word *love* with regard to Agnes, and found it easier to discard other competing emotions and define it in the negative. For sure it had something to do with sex, but my desire for Agnes was also driven by a further wealth of feeling that wasn't affinity, or not merely affinity, nor was it a twinning, although this idea did at least begin to approximate what I was after. There *was* a feeling of twinship, not least because we resembled each other physically, and could have passed for brother and sister. So what was I to make of the fact that it was the death of her real brother that destroyed our marriage? I remembered telling her, in the immediate

36

aftermath of Danny's death, that she would be better off without me, better able to get on with her life. The inadequacy of this as justification for leaving her was made very clear to me. I tried to explain how corrosive it would be, her conviction of my responsibility for Danny's death.

'Then change my conviction,' she said.

I was silent. I opened my hands, a gesture of helplessness. I couldn't do it, I told her. It was during that conversation, or one identical to it — they blur together in my memory now — that I remember her pummeling my chest with her fists, weeping with frustration, and me standing there with my arms by my sides in a posture of stoic mortification.

That was all behind us now. The most potent charge of emotion weakens over time, unless it's repressed. Then it can wreak havoc in the psyche for years to come, which was what had happened to Danny and his buddies. Their buried material was throwing up nightmares and other symptoms, and would continue to do so until the trauma could be translated into a narrative and assimilated into the self; this was our working assumption, Sam Pike's and mine. But Agnes didn't repress. She remembered in vivid detail the events surrounding Danny's death and my own subsequent departure, for it had kept her effectively out of touch with me for seven years.

But the day I buried my mother she had waited for me afterward and then come home with me.

3

My apartment was on the eleventh floor of a building on West Twenty-third Street. After I moved out of Fulton Street I spent a couple of years in a cramped little studio in the Village before moving up to Chelsea. It was a big corner apartment, not as spacious as the apartment on West Eighty-seventh, which by then I knew was going to Walt, but a good-sized two-bedroom with a view of the river and, to the south, all the way down to the twin towers. My living room, the one with the views, had a broad arched opening halfway down and a kitchen at the far end with a counter and high stools. Two walls were given over to bookshelves, floor to ceiling, crammed full and spilling out. There was a good stereo system and some framed reproductions of works by the surrealists, holdovers from my Baltimore days that I'd never troubled to replace. The dining table was always heaped high with papers and journals, and there was no television, much to the frustration of Cassie, who claimed that weekends spent with me were deadly boring, involving as they did a good deal of reading.

Cassie was a clever child with a flair for the dramatic gesture. At times she was distant and dreamy, apparently indifferent to the world around her. She was tall for her age and had a mass of tangled blond hair that would fall across her face like a curtain.

'Daddy, *everybody* has TV! You are such a dinosaur.'

'What sort of a dinosaur, honey?'

She'd roll her eyes in despair. But she was just as happy with a book as she would have been with TV. She only pretended to be a modern child.

Agnes, on her second visit to my apartment, wandered the bookshelves while I ordered food from the Chinese place on Eighth Avenue. She pulled out a volume of Wallace Stevens and idly turned the pages. 'Charlie,' she said, 'you don't imagine I've forgiven you?'

I was still on the phone. I turned toward her. She was wearing a black skirt and a dark blouse of some silky loose material, and she had not yet removed her raincoat. She had changed in the years we'd been apart, somehow become more of a woman, her long, clever face sprinkled with freckles now and a sort of wryness apparent in her slightly snaggletoothed grin. Often she talked with a hand-rolled cigarette hanging from the corner

40

of her mouth, her eyes squinting against the smoke. Her hair still tumbled untidily to her shoulders, much as it had when I first met her. She stood by the bookshelves and took the cigarette from between her lips.

'Because if you do, I have to tell you that it isn't what this is about.'

I was still ordering food, and it was a mark of some intellectual agility on my part that I could sustain both that activity and Agnes's last sentence. I completed the order and put the phone down. I didn't give a damn whether she thought that I thought that she'd forgiven me: she was here. I sat leaning forward on a high kitchen stool, my legs slightly bent and my palms on my thighs.

'Come here at once,' I said.

Agnes, smoking, continued to turn the pages, her face averted from me. I waited. She walked down the room, swaying a little, and tossed the book onto the sofa, where I found it the next morning. I opened my arms, and when she stepped between them I slid my hands in under the raincoat, clasping her slim frame to me with some force. She leaned into me and we kissed. Why was she doing this? Only once had I properly met Leon, her second husband, Cassie's stepfather. Leon O'Connor. They came from the same town on Long Island; apparently they had dated in high school. He worked for the Fire Department.

I remembered the defensiveness in Agnes's tone when I'd asked what he did for a living. We were still enemies in those days but were forced to cooperate for Cassie's sake.

'Yes, you laugh,' she'd said, 'that's just like you.'

'I'm not laughing.'

But a *fireman*? And her with a PhD in sociology? This had been my thought.

'Better a decent fireman,' she'd said.

'Better than what?'

'Than a shit of a shrink.'

By then I had mastered the ability to bite back my anger when she dispensed some particle of her own reservoir of resentment. I hoped the fireman would extinguish some at least of her unhappiness, and for a while it seemed he had. The one time we met, it was because there'd been some miscommunication about when I was supposed to pick up Cassie from Fulton Street. My daughter, then aged five, interposed her body. 'Daddy,' she said, 'this is Leon O'Connor. Leon, this is Daddy.'

Done with grace. She was a precocious child. We shook hands. He was as tall as me and strongly built, a formidable man with cropped hair and a thick, tobacco-stained mustache. New York Irish. But he was not healthy. His skin was gray and he had a ragged cough.

'Hi,' he said.

'Hi.'

Then I thought, what does he see? Some shit of a shrink. The asshole who walked out on Agnes when she needed him most — see *him* climb the stairs of a blazing tenement with sixty pounds of gear on his back to save a kid! Cassie was watching us closely.

'You two going swimming?' Leon O'Connor said.

'Yes, we are, aren't we, Daddy?'

'Sure.'

'You have a good time, sweetheart.'

Sweetheart. He calls my daughter sweetheart. I should have him arrested. I should give him a medal. I should get the fuck out of here. Instead I made conversation.

'You work in the city, Leon?'

'Brooklyn.'

'Why did you go into the Fire Department? You mind my asking?'

'It's what the men in my family do. You kind of take it on board when you're a kid.'

'Never wanted to buck the system?'

'Daddy, can we go now?' She was hopping from foot to foot, suddenly uncomfortable having two daddies in the same room.

43

'Nah. You?'

'Me? Oh, I always wanted to buck the system.'

'Yeah, so I heard.'

In the cab on the way to the pool I pondered that remark. A humbling encounter, but I shouldn't have been surprised. He would have heard Agnes's account, and it wasn't hard to guess how it would play in the moral theater of Leon's mind. A familiar sensation occurred then, and I didn't attempt to suppress it, the welling of anger and within it a flame of resistance: *I did the right thing. Agnes will understand that one day.* At the same time, streaming in like a tide was my acceptance of the inevitability of her version of events, with me at fault, me the shit. What else was this Leon to think of me?

'Daddy, what are you *doing?*'

I realized I was staring out the window of the cab and that my hands, clenched tight on my thighs, had begun furiously kneading the fabric of my trousers. 'Sorry, honey,' I said, 'I was thinking about something else.'

With Agnes that second night I again held back from asking what it meant that she should come to me like this. I had to respect her discretion. But at the same time I wanted to know, and she knew it. Afterward, as she smoked, and again we watched the lights on the ceiling, she said, 'So why don't you ask me? I never knew you to be reticent before, not about things like this.'

'So tell me.'

'It's not what you think.' Suddenly she pushed back the sheet and, swinging her long legs over the side of the bed, sat with her back to me, tapping her cigarette in the ashtray on the night table. Her head sank forward, one hand covering her face. In the gloom I saw her shoulders shaking, but there was no sound. 'What's going on?' I whispered.

My hand was on her spine but she shook me off. She stubbed out the cigarette and left the room. She returned dry-eyed, wrapped in a bath towel that she shed as she got back into bed. 'I don't want to talk about it,' she said.

'You sure about that?'

I loomed over her, peering into her face. Did it still work? Could I read her like I used to? But no, a new layer of emotion had silted and hardened upon what once had been a virgin bed of trust. She may have offered me her body but she wasn't about to give me her heart, not now.

★ ★ ★

Danny never missed a meeting. He was a raw-boned and taciturn man who gave off a

45

strong feeling of separateness. *Don't touch me*, he seemed to say. *Come no closer.* I understood from the others that he'd been a tough soldier who'd watched his buddy die. Something happened to him after that, and four months later they shipped him home.

He seldom talked, and when he did his voice was so low we had to strain to hear him. I never heard that quality of silence in the group at any other time. One night, though, he described how his buddy died. He spoke as if there were a gun to his head, and in a way there was: he had an alien inside his brain, a foreign body he could neither assimilate nor expel. His squad was ambushed out on patrol. When fired on you throw yourself down. His buddy threw himself into the brush beside the path, where a primitive contrivance was waiting for him, a plank of wood with spikes driven up through it. Impaled, horribly injured, he quickly bled to death.

The other men were disgusted. There were loud cries of anger. One remark stayed with me.

'No safe place, man,' said Billy Sullivan, a heavy guy from Staten Island, twenty-five now, who'd served two tours and come back stammering, plagued by nightmares, hands shaking so bad he could barely, at times, so he told us, get the bottle to his lips.

46

No safe place. Danny seemed to have gone on a sustained rampage after that. I think he went berserk. He was lucky to have survived. But it was the aftermath that mattered. In Danny's nightmares, the Vietnamese he'd killed rose up from the earth and came after him. Night after night they came back, night after night he was pursued by the running corpses of his victims until he awoke in sweaty suffocation and could still smell their bodily corruption in the room. Sometimes the smell lingered all day long. Later he talked more about the loss of his buddy. He said he didn't try to replace him, instead he became cold and isolated, embittered to the point of numbness. This grieving man withdrew emotionally, as do all of us who grieve. Robbed of a friendship that had been the one tender sound, the single grace note in the cacophony of violence and insanity and death, he shut down his humanity. Better not to feel.

It was also clear he was drinking heavily, alone, every night, so as to mentally climb down from the state of combat readiness in which he spent most of his waking hours. He couldn't help it. In his mind he was still in the jungle. So his morose, apparently resentful presence was at least in part the function of a chronic hangover. Agnes later confirmed this to me.

Again she came to the hospital, and again we went for a beer. It was a strange relationship we had at first, those stray hours snatched at the end of a long working day. We soon became lovers. I brought her downtown to Walt's loft at the bottom of Chambers Street. I was still living there but it wasn't satisfactory. The facilities were minimal, and with Walt's irregular rhythms of existence I found it difficult to work the long hours demanded of me. They stayed up so late, they made so much noise! There were days when the psych unit seemed a haven of tranquillity by contrast, the company of the mentally ill preferable by far to that of Walt's carousing painter friends.

There had been tension between Walt and me for some months. At first he welcomed Agnes. In those days almost all the females who came through the loft were hippie girls he found it easy to seduce. Painterly mess for some reason never failed to turn them on: trestle tables heaped with squeezed tubes, tools and brushes everywhere, wine bottles, a paint-spattered floor. Three windows faced west toward the river; at the other end of the space the windows faced east to Broadway and south to the near-complete twin towers.

We were close to the site of what once had been the Washington Street produce market. The area was cheap because the Port Authority had recently torn down what it called a commercial slum, actually a viable community of saloons and coffee shops and a few blocks of stores specializing in electronics and radio parts. But by the time I moved back to the city it was mostly artists you saw on the streets down there, painters and sculptors who like Walt had moved into the empty warehouses to take advantage of the light, the high ceilings, the low rent or even no rent at all. So north of Chambers an artist community was in formation, while south was a wasteland where the bulldozer and the wrecking ball had reduced all to rubble, the rubble then dumped into the Hudson for landfill.

Agnes did not at once regard Walt as some kind of bohemian art god, and was not prepared to worship. I'd told her about my disillusionment with his work. There was no *politics*, and what was worse, he didn't see any problem with that, being more passionate about a few square feet of painted canvas than he ever was about the escalation of the war in Vietnam. I remember how impatient I used to get when they started talking art theory, Walt and his friends, I think because I couldn't imagine such talk being treated with anything but contempt by the veterans I knew. The arguments about formalism they pursued deep into the night seemed to me so far beside the point as to be immoral.

Agnes felt as I did, but when she confronted Walt on the apolitical issue he always eluded her. Only once do I remember her cornering him, or at least angering him sufficiently that he exploded, saying he had no time for art that tried to change his mind about the world.

'Who needs it?' he shouted. 'I have a show!'

'That has nothing to do with it.'

Agnes in those days was tenacious, also blunt. Her style was confrontational, and she was impatient with evasion.

'I have to sell the work! Why else would I do it?'

I don't remember her answer exactly. It was along the lines, I think, of a work of art being about more than its commercial viability. Walt stamped around the loft mocking us as sentimental fools. Philistines. *Romantics*, worst of all.

'You probably think art is about beauty!' he shouted.

'No, I don't,' said Agnes.

It was late at night. None of the windows had drapes, so life was lived after dark against huge rectangles of blackness. I remember once discovering on Walt's shelves a book of plates by Goya. It was titled *Los Caprichos*. It contained the drawing beloved by psychiatrists the world over: 'The sleep of reason produces monsters.' Nothing could better express what was happening to America in those years, but I was more interested in another drawing, 'Here comes the bogeyman,' which showed two terrified children clutching their mother's skirt while she gazes up at a cowled and hooded figure standing before her in shadow. Goya's caption says in effect that it is wrong to teach a boy to fear the bogeyman more than he does his father, and thus make him afraid of something that does not exist — *y obligarle a temer lo que no existe*.

The problem in those years was the refusal to recognize a bogeyman that *did* exist, and that ravaged the minds of the men who'd had the misfortune to encounter it, and whose suffering was then compounded by the willful blindness of those who denied its existence. Walter eventually came around to our side, as my mother did. She was as vehement as any of us once she had, but when she first met Agnes she still believed that Nixon was going to end the war.

She'd let things slide after Fred left her.

51

The apartment was always awash in newspapers and discarded clothing and empty glasses. She was a full-time writer by then; she'd come to it late, but her two novels had been respectfully received. One afternoon I took Agnes up there and we found her sitting by the empty fireplace with a book in her lap staring into space. She was a little drunk. She rose with a small cry of pleasure. Agnes knew to expect eccentric behavior. I remember how she gazed at my mother with a curiosity in which I detected no trace of intimidation. Agnes wasn't a woman who could be pushed around, of this I was well aware, but at the same time I'd been accustomed to think of Mom as the force indomitable. I went to the kitchen for drinks, and when I came back the two of them were already arguing about the war. Did we talk of nothing else? Mom was a heavy smoker, and it was wrecking her throat. Her voice was hoarse and scratchy. She was telling Agnes we had to be in Vietnam or all Southeast Asia would be lost.

'Lost to what?' said Agnes.

'To Communist China. That's why your brother went over there.'

'Danny was drafted.'

'At least he didn't burn his draft card.'

'He believed what they told him.'

'And he doesn't now. What a pity.'

'A *pity?*' said Agnes.

My mother was a humped, bent little woman even then, bowed in the shoulders, her spine distinctly curved. She wore a denim shirt and corduroy trousers and a string of large wooden beads. The black hair with its silver streaks was swept back off her forehead.

'Yes, my dear, a *pity*. Such a waste. To make that sacrifice, and then turn against his country.'

'Danny hasn't turned against his country.'

'So what would you call it?' She turned to face Agnes full on, her dark eyes bright and her lip trembling a little.

Agnes gave out one of her small barks of laughter.

'Danny thinks his country's turned against him.'

It was as though she had invoked some sexual practice known only to the most grievously depraved.

Late that night, back at the loft, I sat out on the fire escape by myself watching the lights of the traffic on West Street. I could see Agnes as she sat there staring at Mom, the force indomitable, with no trace of fear. I was much affected by this. I needed a strong woman. Like many in this profession, I had experienced my own need for love as a destructive force. It's what attracts us to the damaged birds, but in Agnes I could see no damage at all.

I came to the conclusion that what had angered me that evening was my mother's attitude to what she'd called Danny's sacrifice, her assumption that he was motivated by a kind of pure, uncomplicated patriotism. There were times when I regarded the pathology of the damaged men I worked with as emblematic of a far greater malaise, and I was apt then to be seduced by my own grand diabolical vision in which America played the part of a mad god eager to devour its young, the willing slave of its own death instinct. Danny wasn't alone in his mute recognition of his damage, and his anger was exacerbated by the recognition that it had occurred in the service of no noble cause. It was meaningless and it was unnecessary, and I saw, every day, that a great part of the difficulty faced by men like him came from having to balance expectations like my mother's with memories of insane slaughter. The irony was that fighting for your country rendered you unfit to be its citizen.

★ ★ ★

Later, when Agnes and I were living together in the apartment on Fulton Street, a few blocks up from the fish market, Danny would show up when he felt the need of human company, or of people, at least, with whom he had more connection than he did with the stranger on the next bar stool. He was no more talkative than when we'd first met. I would like to say that he was getting better. Agnes said she'd seen signs of improvement, but it wasn't the case. The drinking was starting to take a toll. He was usually unshaven, and beneath the stubble his face was coarsely inflamed. He was growing a hard, swollen belly and he had the unmistakably bloated look of an alcoholic. The heavy intake of unfiltered cigarettes had brought on a harsh cough he was unable to shake.

He had keys to the apartment but never once showed up at bad times or stayed too long; the reverse, in fact. He'd shake my hand when he came in and then look around for Cassie, whom he adored. He would lift her high in the air and she'd shriek with laughter when he threatened to drop her, and at times like this I'd watch his face and he seemed a child himself. Agnes saw it too, and we had an odd sense, sometimes, that he was our child, ours to protect, for his pain and vulnerability were heartbreaking. I could tell when he was flashing back to the war. He would sit very still. His mouth fell open and his eyes became glazed and empty, his face masklike. After several seconds, sometimes longer, he came back to the here and now with a shake of the head.

'You want to talk about it?'

'Nah,' he'd say. 'Same old bullshit.'

He was a stoic. I had some idea what this *same old bullshit* looked like. Other times I would see him violently startled by the telephone, or a knock on the door, by one of us coming into the room or Cassie starting to cry. He immediately grew tense, his back stiff, hands gripping the arms of the chair. His eyes darted about the room, calculating where he could find cover, where his back would be protected.

'It's okay, Dan, just a delivery.'

It upset him that this happened. Feeling he'd abused our hospitality, he would leave soon afterward. It was no use trying to stop him. He would suddenly head for the door, and though we offered him the sofa he never took it, he needed to be in the bars for hours yet before sleep would come. At times Agnes went into the bedroom after he'd gone and closed the door behind her, and I could hear her crying in there. It reminded me of my mother, of course, and as with her I would go to Agnes and give what comfort I could. So for the first months of Cassie's life her uncle Danny was a frequent, moody presence in the apartment, but not for a single moment did either of us resent his presence.

This in part was because of his courtesy toward us, and also the dignity that never failed him, at least not in my presence, and which I think derived from a personal code that enabled him to hold on to what few small scraps of self-respect had survived the war. At times I glimpsed what I thought of as the real Danny, like a ghost within the shattered personality. Then he was visible, if only faintly so, and this was what lent such pathos to the man, that you could see what he would've been had the war not traumatized him.

'I'm fucked, Charlie. Don't worry about it.'

But he would never tell me his story, not of what had happened to him those last four months. He was too ashamed, I think, too ashamed of what he'd done. I saw how the men in the group formed a defensive circle around him, emotionally as well as spatially. Danny liked to sit at the back, on the outer edge of the loose, open circle of chairs, close to both the wall and the door. Even when he showed up late nobody took his chair, although for several of those men a seat close to the door was preferable to any other in the room. He paid close attention to what was said, and at times, when some part of another man's experience conformed to his own, he would nod emphatically. This was always remarked on. 'Right, Dan?' the guy would say, and he would lift his head and give consent to what was being said.

Agnes liked it when I talked about Danny, though I rarely had anything to tell her other than that he had showed up. When the meeting ended it was usually late, for we often ran over our two hours into three or even four if we were getting real work done, and it's a mark of how strong their need was that we could talk for so long, and at such a harrowing emotional pitch. Danny always lingered a few minutes at the end, long enough for me to get across the room to him. 'Good meeting,' he'd say, then ask if it was okay for him to stop by on Saturday, and of course I said yes. But he liked to be sure he was expected.

I'd begun to guess what happened those last months in Vietnam, that he'd gone through a worse ordeal than the others and that they knew it too. Later I spent many hours thinking about this, and trying to see what I'd obviously failed to see then. It took me a long time to discover what the missing element was; this is in no way an excuse, but I remember how busy my life was then, those long hours in the psych unit. Agnes did try to persuade me to cut back. She was doing her academic work in the apartment and looking after Cassie at the same time, and it was lonely for her if I didn't get home till eight or nine or later.

By then I was exhausted. I took for granted that she understood all this. My memory is of coming home in the evening and the pair of us then talking at the kitchen table for an hour or so before going to bed. I don't remember any sustained friction, or her voicing any serious objection to being left alone with Cassie. But later she produced a different account, and it's hard to know exactly where the truth lies. There must have been nights we argued, quietly, so as not to wake Cassie, but for me they weren't the dominant feature of those days. Agnes for her part has no strong recollection of a shared sense that we were living useful lives, or that a time would come when we'd have more money, and more time together, and that it would all have been worth it, and so on: the sentiments any couple feels at this stage.

She said later that the deal was unfair, that she'd felt imprisoned in the apartment, that I was selfish and moody. Again, this is not how I remember it, and to me it doesn't sound like Agnes, who was never a passive or put-upon woman. It is my conviction that she revised her memories after the fact so as to bring them into line with her anger. This falsification of memory — the adjustment, abbreviation, invention, even *omission* of experience — is common to us all, it is the business of psychic life, and I was never seriously upset about it. I know how very fickle the human mind is, and how malleable, when it has to accommodate belief, or deny the intolerable.

But it all came back to Danny. He was so important to us, and I have no doubt I allowed Agnes's feelings about him to influence my own attitude. I have often tried to imagine how I might have seen him had he been just one of the guys in the group and not her brother. Certainly he was haunted by repressed memories he hadn't yet found a means of articulating, and he was never able to use the group to find the strength to confront his nightmares sober.

But would I have glamorized him, seen something tough, laconic, even heroic, in a particularly American sort of a way, in his posture of lonely suffering? I believe Agnes's romanticizing her brother influenced me, and that perhaps I failed to appreciate how weak he was. Perhaps I tended to view his isolation as a mark not of fragility but of resilience. Had the question been put to me directly I'm sure I would have said he had no resilience at all, but it never was put to me like that, and I accepted too easily Agnes's picture of the protective elder brother who never let her down, whose courage and recklessness were famous in her hometown, whose readiness to take a beating, when the old man came home drunk, rather than allow him to beat up any of the women in the house, made her cry to think about even years later.

Then, too, the quiet deference of the other guys in the group — it all came together to create a certain image, but I should have seen how much of his core had been blasted, and how unstable what little remained of him actually was. The outward form of the man was still apparent to Agnes, but she didn't suspect how thin a shell it was, that it was as brittle as a wafer. I saw more than she did yet I too failed to recognize the extent of his frailty.

4

In the weeks following my mother's death I
grew increasingly preoccupied with my newly
revived relationship with Agnes. Her reserve
excited me. Her implicit statement that
regions of her being once mine were now
closed to me, this aroused in me a strong urge
to penetrate them. I didn't question it, I
didn't subject this urge of mine to any
imperative of deference, or even of common
civility. I wanted to know what went on in her
mind. What had happened to her while we
were apart? I wanted to be in possession of
the facts. Agnes clearly had ideas of her own
with regard to the scope and depth of this
resurgent liaison, but my intention was to
disregard those limits and break down her
resistance by whatever means necessary.

'Leon doesn't suspect you're having an
affair?' I said one night.

'Charlie, you're not to ask me questions
like that.'

It was the third or fourth time she'd come
to the apartment. Again, it was the happy
hour in the bed after sex when tenderness
and languor and lingering physical pleasure

encourage lovers to reveal all.

'What would happen if he found out?'

'If you don't stop, I won't come here again.'

'It's not so odd that I should ask, is it?'

'I know what you're doing, so just quit it.'

'What I'm doing is very simple. I just want to know what this is all about.'

'You don't like it? Relax, Charlie. Stop thinking.'

The idea of stopping thinking struck me as amusing. I knew Agnes knew she was being unreasonable by refusing to disclose any motive or explanation, but I also knew she knew my curiosity would not be bound by the normal parameters, that in this regard I was not a normal man: I was a psychiatrist. She knew my need to excavate far beyond what was comfortable, beyond what was even reasonable, logical or comprehensible. But she wouldn't allow the door to open so much as a crack, and while this frustrated me it also became a source of keen intrigue.

'I wonder if what you want is that I uncover what you're hiding by means of your body.'

I wasn't altogether clear what I meant by this. I had been reading about a theory of memory that rejected the idea of storage and instead posited memory as dynamic somatic imprinting.

'Charlie!'

'Your resistance is almost pathological.'

At this she walked out of the bedroom. A few minutes later I was standing in the hallway in my bathrobe, where I at least made an attempt at amends.

'Okay, I was being psychiatric. I'm sorry.'

But she came back. It wasn't as though we had nothing else to talk about. There was Cassie, who according to Agnes became more precocious and more eccentric every day; more difficult, she meant. She was worried, and I tried to tell her that our daughter was simply growing up, becoming an individual. I didn't ask her about our daughter's relationship with Leon, which I strongly suspected was turbulent, Cassie being of an age now to fall in love with her real daddy — me — and treat my rival with breezy disdain. We talked about Agnes's sister, Maureen, the one-time hippie earth mother who now ran a secondhand bookstore on Fourth Avenue; and of course about her brother. About Danny's suicide, and Agnes's gradual change of heart in this regard — her acceptance of the idea that I couldn't have prevented it, that it would have happened anyway. Probably. I was surprised by this, and heartened.

'But then to leave me!'

For once I didn't challenge her, although I

still believed I'd been right to leave. Instead, tentatively, I asked whether her changed attitude regarding my responsibility for Danny's death was what had made her wait for me after my mother's funeral, and kept bringing her back to my apartment. I didn't know if this would anger her.

'Of course it did. You think I'd come here if I hated you?'

'So do you love me?'

'Don't get carried away, Charlie. All I said was, I didn't hate you. I *did* hate you, but I don't now. It's such hard work hating someone.'

'I've never hated anyone. Except my father. And Walt, of course, but that's complicated. That's not true hatred.'

'What is it then?'

'You want me to tell you a story about Walt?'

I was watching her closely. Did she want me to tell her a story about Walt? I took a strong interest in what others felt about my brother, and it was a source of astonishment to me that people didn't see right through him. When Agnes first met him, Walt was a hairy, hard-drinking painter-man whose abstract aesthetics were tempered by a ferocious ambition he did little to conceal. This wasn't something I could talk to him about. Walt derided me for supposedly upholding some outdated myth of the artist in the garret, and I told him that his cynicism made a mockery of any aspiration to integrity he might claim. On one occasion, and this was the story I told Agnes, I had accused him of being indifferent to the war — this at a time when the streets of American cities were loud with protest. Walt's response was extraordinary. He claimed he was himself at war.

'At war with what?' I'd said.

'With the history of art.'

I had never forgotten it. I told Agnes about it as though it had happened not years ago but yesterday.

'You do know, don't you, that you've told me that story before?' she said.

I was aware that I'd told her the story before, but what mattered was that she share my horrified amusement. So deep an impression had it made on me, so strong was the charge that still attached to the memory, that it overrode any embarrassment I may have felt about repeating myself.

'Oh, Charlie, you're so odd about Walter. I'm afraid your mother's responsible for that.'

'You think it's unhealthy.'

'Sure I think it's unhealthy. I never figured out why she treated you so badly, and so adored Walter.'

This, too, we'd discussed before. The sad fact was, I didn't know either.

'But you're the shrink!'

I spread my hands wide. *I didn't know.*

One night, when she was about to return to Fulton Street, I asked why she couldn't stay the night.

'Don't, Charlie. Try to imagine my situation. It's not easy.'

I said nothing. She put her arms on my shoulders. She was almost as tall as me in her heels.

'You're a nice guy,' she said. 'Say something, Charlie. Be nice.'

'I'm running on empty here,' I said.

She angled her head slightly and kissed me.

'Is it very unfair?' she said.

'I think it is.' She gazed at me then with what looked like sadness tinged with affection, but said nothing.

A little later I sat in the dark apartment feeling like a man suffering from a peculiar sort of thirst. Lacking the power to control the course of the relationship, starved of information about what was happening in Fulton Street and forced to accommodate Agnes's erratic schedule, I was in the position of a kept man. Concubinage was still a criminal offense in some countries. Sophia Loren had been prosecuted for it. Of course I wasn't *paid* to hold myself in readiness for my lover's occasional appearances, unless the sex was itself payment; and there were the women I visited on Lexington Avenue and elsewhere, though they offered little of what I required, the sort of intimacy that Agnes promised but never quite delivered. She never stayed the night and gave me only partial glimpses of the life she led apart from me. But despite my dissatisfaction I knew it wouldn't be me who broke off the arrangement. I still entertained fantasies of the three of us living under one roof, a family. And god knows I needed a family — my own had been a disaster.

★   ★   ★

After she'd left, my mind drifted back to the story I'd told her about Walter. The bond between brothers is often intense, but it isn't necessarily affection that unites them. Affection was rarely evident in our relationship, yet we depended on each other in a number of ways. I often questioned him closely about our childhood. Being three years older than me, he remembered more than I could, and despite the patent unreliability of such memories I was always eager to hear his stories. I remember one particular conversation in some detail. We were sitting up late drinking in my apartment.

'Did he ever have a job?' I said.

We were talking about Fred, of course.

'He brought in a little cash now and then, but it was never clear where he got it. Gambling, I guess, the horses. I think he fenced stolen property, but very small-time. You remember that time the bedroom was full of cardboard boxes?'

'No.'

'I had a look in one of them. Kitchen equipment. Egg beaters, knives and forks, pots and pans. Mom told him if he didn't get that shit out of the apartment she'd call the cops.'

I think I would've looked more kindly on my father's shortcomings, or with less scorn, at least, if he'd been even slightly affable or affectionate toward me. But he wasn't.

'You remember how he'd just *blow?*' said Walt.

Oh, I remembered. I remembered him shouting, I remembered doors being slammed, plates and glasses being smashed. I remembered how once I climbed onto the table and sang 'The Star-Spangled Banner' with my hand on my heart, just to distract him. It worked: the astonishment was enough to disrupt his anger and turn it into laughter. Walter nodded when I told him this story. He'd been there, of course; in fact he'd probably shaped the story for me in later years.

'Why did he get so mad?' I said.

Adult anger is terrifying to a child. The loss of control threatens the stability of his world and puts him in fear of his life. The child has no confidence in his ability to withstand rage, and believes it will break him into fragments.

'Because Mom told him he was a loser.'

'You heard her say that?'

'Not in so many words.'

'Then how do you know?'

'Christ, Charlie, I just remember how she'd go for his jugular, and it drove him crazy.'

Fred Weir in fact *was* a loser, and this must have been apparent to others long before I realized it myself. My mother, on the other hand, was a sharp-tongued woman who saw no reason not to speak her mind, which made her ill-suited for life with a lazy, shiftless, short-tempered man like him. Small wonder that as a child I used to dream of him putting a gun to my head and threatening to kill me.

'She provoked him, didn't she?' I said.

'He couldn't take criticism. She didn't care. She wasn't going to keep quiet just because he lost his temper.'

Walter fished a cigar out of his pocket and took a moment to get it going. I waited.

'It got pretty bad at times,' he said.

'What do you mean?'

'He used to hit her.'

He leaned across the table and refilled my glass. I didn't remember it, but at the same time I knew it had happened. Nobody had ever told me it happened, but I was sure that when he described it I would recognize it. In fact, I could dimly visualize it already. I said as much.

'I guess you've wiped it. I wish I could.'

'Why?'

'I saw it happen one time. He knocked her down, but she got right back up like one of those dolls and called him a cocksucker and then *boom!* Down she went again.'

'Where did it happen?'

'In some hotel in the Catskills. I saw it through a crack in the door. I never told her I saw him hit her. Then he'd walk out and we'd hear her crying in there. You hated that. You'd go in and try to comfort her.'

'I do remember that.'

'But this one time it was really bad.'

'Go on.'

'You remember his gun?'

His gun. Fred and his firearms.

'No.'

But I did, and even as I denied it I felt the memory begin to stir, the dream of the gun rising in my mind as though from under a

71

lifting mist — it was what I'd felt a moment before, the certainty that when he said it I would know it. Fred's gun, which he kept in a locked drawer of his desk in the living room. But Walter knew where he put the key: on the top shelf of a cupboard in the kitchen. One time, when Fred was out, and Mom was in her room, we unlocked the drawer and looked at the gun. It lay there among the bills and checkbooks, a heavy black automatic. His service weapon from World War II. Neither of us dared even touch it. Fred always had firearms. He went to jail for firearms.

'So what about the gun?'

'Oh, I forget now. All so long ago.'

5

Then my life changed. It was sudden, and while it took me by surprise, in retrospect I see that I had been unconsciously preparing myself for just such an event. I met a woman. Her name was Nora Chiara. Now I should tell you at once that by this time in my life I was not a catch. On a busy street in Manhattan your eye would not be drawn to this harried-looking figure, above medium height, conservatively dressed and older, apparently, than his almost forty years. I had a failed marriage behind me, I lived for my work, I never left town, and the people I saw most often were my daughter and my brother and his family, who'd moved into the apartment on Eighty-seventh Street left to them by my mother.

The first time I saw her she was in a restaurant called Sulfur, one of the new places then opening downtown. It was popular in those days and may be still for all I know, but it always reminded me of a railroad station. The noise of so many people beneath so high a ceiling made me think of trains, or of *missing* trains. The fear of missing trains. I was in private practice by then and had a small office on Park Avenue. One of my patients at the time, Joseph Stein, dreamed of missing trains, and this is why I mention it, for he was on my mind that night: this was a man who through no fault of his own had killed a pedestrian when he'd lost control of his car on an icy road. Having taken a life he didn't know why he himself should be allowed to live, and this was causing me some concern. We had established trust, and what I was trying to elicit from him now was the trauma story itself: what happened, what were the details of the thing, what did he feel, what did his body do, what did it all mean. Only when we had the trauma story, and he'd assimilated it into conscious memory — into the *self* — could we move on to the last stage, which involved reconnecting him to the world, specifically his family and the community in which he lived.

There was a long bar of dark wood, the open cabinets behind it rising to the ceiling and stacked with bottles of red wine that gleamed black as billiard balls. You could sit at the counter and eat hard-boiled eggs with your wine, if you wanted to. From the ceiling, large yellow globe-lamps spread a penumbral half-light on the scattering of tables on the mosaic tile floor far below.

That night, a wet night in early April, I'd been supposed to dine with Walt but he canceled at the last minute. I was already downtown, so rather than go back to Twenty-third Street I'd come in out of the rain and asked for a table for one. I was seated in the corner, and over my newspaper I watched the owner's wife, Audrey, pull up a chair at a noisy table and engage in a low-voiced conversation with a small, dark-haired woman I'd noticed the moment I stepped into the place. I guessed she was in her early thirties. She possessed the sort of beauty I associate with French actresses of a certain age, and she gave off a faint, subtle suggestion of recent grievous suffering. Her heart had been much broken; or so one felt, watching her.

I ordered a salad and a piece of grilled fish. At first I thought she must be a celebrity of some kind, though in this I was mistaken. She was famous only for destroying men. That night she wore a dark gray cashmere shawl around her shoulders, also an air of distant indulgence, laughing occasionally but giving the impression that this was a mere flurry on a sea of private pain. She was attached to nobody, yet they all in a way performed for her. Only her friend Audrey seemed able to bring a spark of life to her gravely composed features. I watched her with some curiosity, for if it was a performance — as I assume all public behavior is, at root — then its accomplishment was to seem anything but, which perhaps was why the entire table sought to amuse her.

She didn't move from her place — no table-hopping for this one — and sustained her composure throughout the evening; and when the table began to break up she showed no effects of the wine she'd drunk, six glasses of Chablis by my count. I watched her as she paused at the door for a last word with her friend. She touched the other woman's cheek and murmured what looked like 'Bless you,' then disappeared into the night.

Then, a week later, quite by chance, or at least I assumed it was, I encountered her again. Walt had asked me to dinner to make up for the evening we'd missed at Sulfur. It had been a long day. Joe Stein was beginning to display a fixation on his trauma, a worrying development. He told me that his mental life was now entirely focused on the death of the pedestrian. When his wife called to remind him of his mother's birthday, he at once thought of the birthday of the mother of the man who'd died, and then of the dead man's birthday, or rather of the fact that for him there would be no more birthdays, and why?

Because — and so he was back to it.

'Because I killed the poor bastard!'

Stein was a slim, bald, dapper little man, a commodities broker with an office on Wall Street. The trauma was obsessing him. He was starting to structure his entire mental life around it. Not good. Not uncommon, but not good. So I really wasn't in the mood for company, but Walt had insisted. There was someone he wanted me to meet. I left my apartment with some irritation, but managed to find a cab right away. The driver was from the Soviet Union.

'You want the highway, you want local?'

'Highway.'

Night was falling. Stein had told me he was thinking about suicide. Though I was fairly sure he didn't mean it, I'd been wrong before. I remember staring out at the river and imagining him jumping from the George Washington Bridge, then listing all the reasons why that wasn't going to happen. For one thing, he had the support of his wife, and while this may be heresy in my profession, it is often by means of simple courage and a good woman that psychological problems are overcome, and without any help from people like me.

By the time I got out of the cab I'd succeeded in putting all thoughts of suicide out of my mind. I stood outside what I still thought of as my mother's building and gazed down the block to the park, where the trees massed in the now-fallen darkness. A misty rain had begun to fall, slanting through the streetlights. It was one of those deceptively still, mild nights that occasionally occurs in New York, when the city seems to collapse, exhausted from its relentless roaring and surging, and pauses briefly to gather its immense energies before starting up again. What I really wanted was to find some little place on Columbus Avenue and have dinner alone.

Walt, wearing a striped apron, opened the door of the apartment with a glass of wine in his hand. He liked to cook now. He considered himself a nurturing man. He was a good thirty pounds overweight.

'Doctor Charlie,' he said.

He put his hand on my shoulder and we walked down the hall, whose walls fairly bristled with art and into the big atelier, what had once been our living room, the high windows shaded by pale slatted blinds now and a large Twombly hanging over the fireplace. As I came into the room Lucia, Walt's wife, shouted to me from the kitchen, and I caught a glimpse of their eldest child, Jake. A man and two women were sitting on the sofa. To my astonishment the dark-haired woman, the one I'd seen in Sulfur, was one of them.

'Charlie, a good friend of mine, Nora Chiara.'

I almost said, *But I know you.*

★　★　★

I couldn't define her. I knew she was vulnerable. Despite the tough, urbane cast of the woman, the mature intelligence, the sophistication — the whiskey-throated laughter — she was certainly vulnerable. We are all of course *vulnerable*, and I can't pretend that I didn't see it at once, or draw the obvious inference regarding our mutual attraction. There were a number of indications. The twitching foot, or rather the anxiety it couldn't mask, this suggested damage. She had reached for my hand without rising from the sofa, and I'd known then, or thought I did, why Walt had asked me to come: his so-called nurturing included getting me hooked up again. Her gleaming hair was blue-black and cut in a clean line at chin level, exposing the back of her neck and her soft throat. She was wearing a clingy black dress and her shoulders were bare. How small she was, how perfect the swell of her breasts against the black material. How creamy and white her skin. She half-turned on the sofa, an arm thrown over the back, and looked me over rather coolly. She wasn't French, as I'd idly imagined, she was from Queens. I thought of the cashmere shawl that had covered those shoulders and breasts a week ago. I myself was in a gray suit and a black shirt, and by chance a tie the exact same shade as that shawl.

'So you're the shrink,' she said.

'I'm a psychiatrist.'

There was a sort of sharpened gleam about her, as though she sniffed conflict and liked it. For a second I glimpsed her teeth, small and feral, very white against the red lipstick.

'Psychiatrist, then.'

She was certainly direct. Her legs were elegantly crossed at the knee but there was a slight tremor in the lifted foot with its vertiginous stiletto. Her black stockings were sheer, with a seam, and her skirt was riding high on her thighs. And I, freighted with my narcissistic need to be the fixer, the healer, of course I was attracted to her. Moth to a flame. So I did not go in blind.

But the next day, waiting for Stein in my office, when I tried to describe her to myself I had some difficulty, and I'm someone who describes people to himself for a living. I had a couch in the office, an old chesterfield from my Johns Hopkins days, a commodious piece of furniture upholstered in oxblood leather much cracked and creased, and very comfortable. I stretched out on it and closed my eyes. A host of vivid impressions arose which I will not catalog here, apart from this. We'd got out of the cab and were walking toward my building. The night was wet and windy, my arm was around her shoulders, hers around my waist, and we nearly stumbled. 'Fuck,' she shouted, 'these heels!' — but I saw quite clearly what had happened. She'd been trying to avoid a crack in the sidewalk. She wouldn't step on it. It was a fleeting thing, but it stayed with me: a brief glimpse of childish superstition in this very grown-up woman.

When I rose from the couch and prepared for my appointment with Joe Stein I was aware of new feelings stirring in me. Hope, for one.

★　★　★

We decided, that night, to meet in a restaurant. The decorum required in a public place would allow us to negotiate the tricky currents of this unknown sea, this sudden other person. There is trepidation attached to an intimacy embarked on without warning or preparation. Neither of us wanted to go to Sulfur, so I suggested a place in the West Village.

She was wearing a short black jacket over a man's white shirt unbuttoned to her breasts, and a short black skirt. Her hair was slicked back with some sort of gel, and she wore glasses with heavy black frames. Bare legs, black shoes with low heels. I told her later that she looked like a librarian with a secret. Later still I told her she was wanton. But first we had to get through dinner. When she first came into the restaurant I'd watched with quickened heartbeat as she spoke to the waiter, who'd turned to point at where I was waiting with my arm uplifted in the shadows at the back of the room. As I rose with stiffening penis to greet her, she paused, then kissed me lightly on the lips. She was fragrant.

'I couldn't see you,' she said. 'It's like a crypt in here.'

'Are you all right?' I said.

She'd sat down and was dealing with her bag, frowning, sighing, but at this question she grew still and gazed at me. I was saying, Do you regret last night? The sex had been, for me, at least, deeply interesting. She was a restrained lover, almost to the point of passivity: a small, pale, fleshy, pliant doll of a woman in bed, but she talked throughout, which I liked, husky, dirty talk. She had excited a strange fierceness in me that I didn't trouble to analyze. Sex is sex, after all; there are few rules. Do no harm.

'I'm fine, Charlie. How are you?'

I told her I was all right too. We sat in silence until the waiter arrived, drinks were ordered, menus scrutinized.

'I'm starving,' she said.

I thought at first she was just going through the motions, having dinner with me to be polite. And that that would be the end of it. She was behaving not like the vampy creature who'd flirted with me at Walt's, then spent the night in my bed; rather, she was the demure woman I'd seen that evening in Sulfur. But after several glasses of wine she began to warm up. She was with me because she wanted to be, and remembering how we were then, when it was all promise, with nothing to ruin it but folly, or fear, I see us as though from a camera attached to a track on the ceiling: a lean, lanky man with his hair cut short, *en brosse*, in a creased linen suit with one elbow propped on the candlelit table, his chin cupped in his fingers, the other arm thrown over the back of his chair, listening with a smile to this peachy woman gesticulating and smoking on the other side of the table. She ate only a little of her pasta and barely touched her steak. She drank several carafes of white wine, I didn't count, while I nursed a glass of red. She must have smoked seven cigarettes over the course of the meal, but a number of them she crushed out after only one or two drags. I idly wondered why some cigarettes got smoked right down to the filter and others were crushed out at birth.

I paid the check and we emerged into the night. We were a couple of blocks west of Seventh Avenue. She took my hand. We stepped away from the restaurant, and there were flowers for sale in the deli on the corner. I asked her if she'd like some.

'No, Charlie,' she said. 'Let's just go home.'

Home. My apartment, she meant. Which no woman had entered for many months, excepting Agnes, of course. In which I had become accustomed to retire from the world at the end of the day and there indulge the stark pleasures of my solitude. I experienced a flicker of misgiving at the prospect of relinquishing that solitude, but it was only a flicker. For a woman to refer to a man's apartment as home is of some importance, for it suggests trust; and this had come from a woman I'd known barely twenty-four hours. One of the rewards of maturity, I told myself, in a rare burst of complacency, is the ability to make a rapid decision on a matter of profound emotional significance and have confidence in its soundness. The folly in this line of thinking didn't become apparent until later, though even then I was aware, somewhere in the engine room at the back of my mind, of a needle flickering across a gauge and entering the red zone, signaling danger.

Had I guessed it already, had I glimpsed again the eternal inexorable truth that it is always the sick ones who seek out the healers? The lost ones who hunt down the fathers? There was a slight tremor, this I do remember, for I had barely touched my wine, I was clearheaded; or no, not a tremor, a sensation of *blur*, the lover blurring into the shrink. This I ignored, and instead I exulted. Home, such as it was.

★ ★ ★

We could talk, this was the point. In the back of cabs, in restaurants, in the park after visits to Walter and Lucia, all that spring and into the summer we talked, we told each other stories, the stories of our lives so far. Oh, the risks one has run, the injuries suffered, the losses, the triumphs, the vital relationships — though she wouldn't talk about her childhood, curiously — all assume fresh coloring when narrated to a new lover while submerged in her gaze. She was curious about my relationship with Walter. I asked her if she had a sibling, someone she could look up to as I did my brother. I was being ironic.

She shook her head. 'I'm an only child.'

Our conversations were like sex, our sex like conversation. In my relative social isolation since the end of my marriage I'd grown wary and suspicious but now I relaxed; I allowed the inner man to show, whoever he was. Though of course one edits. I spoke little about Agnes, for my relationship with her remained a private affair that would have deeply hurt Nora had she ever found out about it, I mean that Agnes and I continued to meet as we did. For sex. About Danny I spoke still less; in fact, about him I said nothing at all, for his was not a story I could yet trust myself to tell her with any degree of coherence. It was too tragic, too much about futility, about meaningless sacrifice, about violence, about violent death. And while so much of my work involved the pathology of the mind, the tenor of my relationship with Nora Chiara, by contrast, was one of lightness and even, yes, at times, of joy.

I did talk to her about Cassie. I found it impossible not to. I very much wanted them to meet, but Nora resisted the idea. She said there was no point in her becoming friends with my daughter until we knew how we ourselves were going to work out. This was sensible, I supposed, though I was sorry not to be able to introduce her to the child I was so proud of. So on the days I spent with Cassie, Nora worked in the library, and in the end they never met. But I noted with pleasure that they were far from indifferent to each other. When Cassie was in the apartment she inspected whatever clothes Nora had left lying around, being at the age when fashion first becomes interesting to a girl; and Nora was no less curious about Cass. At such times I briefly glimpsed a distinctly maternal aspect that in her seemed surprising.

6

One Sunday afternoon in May we took a walk in Central Park. It was a cool, pleasant day. Recklessly we picked our way through spent needles and dog shit to the Bethesda Fountain, where we sat on a bench so she could smoke a cigarette. Her cheeks were pink from the exertion. My arm was draped over her shoulders as we watched a group of feral children chase one another around the fountain, screaming obscenities. I asked if we could drop in on Walter. I told her I was worried about the safety of my mother's furniture.

'Why wouldn't it be safe?' she said.

'Walter's moved it down to the basement. I don't think he takes much interest. I should get it, by rights. Nobody else wants it.'

'Then ask him for it.'

'It's more complicated than that.'

'I know he'd be happy to have you take it.'

How could she know this? I let it pass; it was the sort of thoughtless thing lovers say to each other all the time. Still, an alarm was sounded. I knew what Walter was like.

Lucia greeted us at the door. She was a

warm, loud, untidy woman who'd come here from Milan some years before to work in the art world, but had instead fallen into the clutches of Walter Weir and borne him four children. My brother didn't deserve her.

'Charlie,' she said tenderly, 'and Nora. Come in.'

She kissed us on both cheeks. We walked down the hall to the kitchen. Her arm was around my waist, her hip plump against mine. One of the children shouted at me from the living room.

'Hi, Uncle Charlie!'

Walt was at the stove wearing that apron of his and smoking a cigar. He was wielding a large steel spatula that dripped hot fat. He thrust it into a skillet and put down his cigar, then came and took me in his arms.

'So glad, buddy,' he murmured in my ear.

He meant me and Nora, our transparent pleasure in each other. I looked around. Great changes had been made. Our mother had never run a clean kitchen. The woodwork of her cupboards and counters were alive with bacteria, and it had long been a joke between us that you ate here, the Grand Central of botulism, at risk of your life. Now all was stainless steel and butcher block, and a hanging metal frame from whose hooks Walt's various copper-bottomed pots and pans dangled like so many weapons. There was an island, as Walt called it, and we sat round it on high stools as he poured us each a glass of what he claimed was one of the great unsung heroes of Burgundy.

'Try this,' he said, 'and tell me it doesn't break your heart. You're staying for supper, by the way. No argument.'

Walt and Lucia's boy Jake was just a year older than Cassie, and there were two younger girls and a baby only a few months old. She was in some sort of basket on the kitchen floor, kicking and gurgling. One of her sisters shuffled into the kitchen. This was Giulia, an ethereal, golden-haired little creature dressed for ballet in tutu and tights, also wearing a pair of her mother's shoes. She peered at her baby sister for a few seconds, then clomped away in her oversized shoes. We chatted for a minute or two and then I said I wanted to have a look at Mom's furniture. Walt gave me the basement keys. 'You want me to come down with you?' he said.

I told him I knew the way. I wanted to go down alone. I knew it would be difficult for me to look at her things with equanimity, particularly seeing them among other tenants' abandoned possessions, objects no longer of use or value in the world of the living.

The basement was reached by a metal stairwell from a door at the back of the lobby. It was dark. Bulbs hadn't been replaced, dust and cobwebs abounded and the clutter of detritus I found when I unlocked the door at the bottom of the stairs — rusted tools, bicycles, cans of gasoline, untidy trays of rat poison, boxes of mildewed clothes — would've made a city inspector slap an injunction on the building in a second. The junk blocked the passageways between the fenced pens where trunks and file cabinets and such had been displaced and forgotten like so many bad memories.

Mom's stuff was in the very back. It was cold down there and the floor shook whenever an A train came rushing through the nearby tunnel. The air smelled stale and faintly rancid. It would have been a dull-witted psychiatrist who failed to recognize this as a representation of the unconscious mind as we knew it, as we encountered its manifest products in our consulting rooms. All her belongings had been handled care-lessly, and no attempt had been made to protect the huge old bed with the carved teak headboard, which had come down through generations of the Hallam family and was now piled high with boxes, chairs, luggage and pictures. I realized at once that if it wasn't soon protected from dust and rodents — from time, neglect, predation — it wouldn't be worth storing at all.

Walt opened the door when I returned to the apartment, and I told him I was going to see to it that everything was properly wrapped in those protective blankets they used.

'You go right ahead,' he said. 'Have them send the bill here.'

In the kitchen they were still drinking wine. I sat down next to Nora. She leaned over toward me and put her hand on mine but kept her eyes on Walt, who was telling a story. I asked them how they'd met each other; Nora had told me once, but I'd forgotten. It turned out that the book she was working on — she was a freelance art researcher — involved a notoriously difficult critic Walter knew when he was starting out.

'She handled him beautifully,' he said. 'Max Green. Such a tricky guy. Such a prick. He'd come to your space and just watch you. He never said anything. He'd let gaps open up in a conversation, just to unsettle you. We don't like silence, people will say anything, then he'd have the advantage. He was like a shrink that way. That's why I introduced you two.'

He was drunk. He grinned at me.

I disliked these half-playful barbs of his. 'So it was all your doing,' I said.

'Charlie, I look out for you.'

He lifted his wineglass to his lips and gazed at me as he drank. Why, so often, this veiled hostility? What had I ever done to him? I glanced at Lucia, who was busy with the pasta. It still worried me that I'd first seen Nora the night Walt had failed to show up at Sulfur, then a week later there she was in his apartment. Freud said there was no such thing as an accident, and this coincidence was odd. I hadn't made sense of it. Perhaps there was no sense to make.

'Walt looks out for everybody,' Nora said.

'Mostly himself,' said Lucia, without turning.

Walt shouted with laughter and slapped the counter. His taking himself no more seriously than he did anybody else could be disarming. He had a beard then, and with his broad face and his tangle of dark hair, he had an aura about him, at least when he was drinking and at ease, that to me suggested some shaggy wine-god figure of dissolute antiquity — cunning as he was genial, entirely lacking in moral scruple, and not for a moment to be trusted, particularly by the brother for whom he sustained this intermittent, inexplicable animosity. Jake, his long-haired and painfully shy son, came in to bum a cookie, and Walter reached into the cupboard for a tin of biscotti. Lucia protested, saying he should wait for dinner. So it went, and we sat sipping Walter's wine and I felt as though I was wrapped in a wool blanket. But just before the food was taken into the dining room Lucia stood before me and took my hands.

'Charlie,' she said gravely, 'we have something to tell you.'

I was alarmed. 'What is it? Tell me at once.'

'Walter has accepted a residency in Venice.'

'For how long?'

'A year.'

'A year! You're all going?'

'Yes, Charlie,' she said. 'It's what I want. I want to see my children in Italy. I want to hear them speak my language.'

'I see.'

'But this is exciting,' said Nora.

A few minutes later we were at the table, where I tried to digest this new development while the children peppered their mother with questions about Italy. Walter turned to me and asked what was wrong. He knew me well.

'This Venice thing,' I said. 'I feel very ambivalent about it.'

'What do you mean?'

94

I shook my head. I didn't want to say it.

'I'll be back now and then,' he said. 'I won't just disappear.'

* * *

Later we took the train back down to Twenty-third. My mood was troubled. I became preoccupied with what I perceived as Walt's cavalier attitude to our mother's possessions, this careless consignment of her furniture to the basement. I couldn't see it as anything other than hostile, or worse, he must hate her, I thought, to behave with such disregard, and he must be aware too of the effect on *me*. Thinking this, I became angry. Nora asked me what was going on, and when I told her she was incredulous.

'Oh, *Charlie*!' she cried.

She wheeled around to face me, and other passengers in the subway car threw shifty glances in our direction before staring back down at the floor.

'Charlie, that's absurd,' she said quietly.

'Is it?'

'Of course it is! Walt just doesn't like old stuff. He has an aesthetic. He has his own taste.'

'And I don't?'

'That's not what I said.'

I stretched my legs out and crossed them at the ankles. I folded my arms and sank my chin onto my chest and I too then gazed unseeing at the floor of the subway car.

Nora thrust her arm through mine. 'You're being ridiculous,' she whispered. 'Everybody gets rid of their mother's furniture. It's not a mark of disrespect. It's just *furniture*.'

She shook her head in disbelief and looked away. I said nothing. There are times when the psychiatric perspective is a liability. You see so much more clearly than those around you the sources and motives of the behavior of others. Nora saw Walt as an artist, as a man with an aesthetic. I saw him as an older brother, threatened, attacking me where he knew me to be most vulnerable: on the maternal front. But I didn't know how to say this to Nora without sounding paranoid. Probably better to say nothing.

'He's persecuting me,' I said.

Her arm was swiftly withdrawn, and again she stared at me aghast. 'Are you *serious?*'

Yes, better to say nothing at all.

'I said, are you serious?'

'It's difficult,' I said, 'for an only child like you to understand what goes on in a family like mine. I think he's not even aware of what he's doing. But you see, my darling, that doesn't mean he's *not* doing it.'

She pulled away from me and sat on the edge of the subway seat, her eyes narrowed and her lips pressed tight together. We were approaching Twenty-third Street. A bag lady shuffled through the car, wheezing and mumbling, her world stuffed into two straining trash bags. A cop with a dog was standing at the far end of the car. The wheels screamed as the train braked into the station. Several passengers rose to their feet.

'Our stop,' I said.

Out on the street she had still said nothing. We were in the elevator of my building when at last she spoke.

'But is it worth it, Charlie?'

'Is what worth it?'

'Constructing these dramas, all this imaginary conflict? It makes everything so fucking complicated.'

'Not imaginary, babe, just concealed. You deny the unconscious?'

'Oh, I don't know! No, I suppose not, but can't you just give it up on Sundays?'

This was a novel thought. We walked down the hall to the door of 11F and I took out my keys. I unlocked both locks, then the dead bolt, and pushed open the door for her. Couldn't I just give it up on Sundays!

'Why not?' I said.

'Why not what?'

97

She was standing in the middle of the room, lighting a cigarette. She was wearing a belted black sweater, close-fitting over breasts and hips. She was still irritated, and what I wanted to do was sweep it away and return us to that easy affectionate spontaneity we'd grown used to.

'Why *not* give it up on Sundays? The unconscious and all its dark works.'

'Yes, Charlie, renounce it!'

Then she was standing in front of me, laughing, her arms outstretched as though in welcome.

'I renounce it,' I said.

Later, it occurred to me that my anger had nothing to do with the furniture. It was about Walt and his family going away for a year. I'd simply displaced the anger, unwilling to acknowledge how much I resented being abandoned.

7

It was late May when Nora moved in with me. She needed a home. For some months she'd been house-sitting a small apartment in the Village, and when the tenant returned to the city she'd moved in with Audrey. She told me she hadn't had a place of her own since her divorce four years earlier, and I was still a little confused as to her source of income, for this freelance research seemed to bring in almost nothing. I was able to create enough closet space for her wardrobe, which was less extensive than I'd feared it would be, but the housing of her books and papers was more problematic. She did much of her work in various libraries around town, though for the actual writing — she still used a manual typewriter, she said she couldn't work any other way — she required a room of her own. I gave her my study, though sometimes she worked at the dining table because she wanted to look out the window at the river.

I liked the sight of a writer's table, books and papers spread across a working surface, pencils, spectacles, typewriter. When I was very young I thought this would be my work, but I am far too social an animal. I require others. I require talk. Every psychiatrist a writer manqué, exiled from the kingdom because he has to talk.

'Charlie, you're early.'

She would shuffle her books and papers together, carry them out and stash them in the spare room. I told her I wanted her to stay where she was, that I liked to see her working. I liked her with her spectacles on.

'Too bad. Pour me a glass of wine.'

Other times she worked all day in the spare room, and when I came home and heard the tapping of her typewriter I'd stand outside the door and allow the sound to arouse memories of my childhood. She emerged once and found me absorbed in nostalgia and asked what I was doing. When I told her she was astonished.

'You think I'm like your mother?'

'Babe,' I said, 'nobody's like my mother and you least of all.'

I was not being entirely candid here. Nora reminded me strongly of my mother, and not just by the sound of her typewriter.

I liked too the evenings we spent together in the kitchen. I liked the ritual of preparing dinner, this an aspect of domestic life that was new to me. When I was married to Agnes I was almost never home in time for dinner, and on West Eighty-seventh Street, especially after Fred ran off with his girlfriend, it was mostly takeout or restaurants.

I took a strong interest in what happened in the kitchen. I asked her questions. Why coriander and not parsley? Why high heat rather than low? Why lemon juice? Why chicken stock? Why simmer? Why must it sit in the fridge overnight? It would have driven another woman crazy but it gave us something to argue about, and arguing, as opposed to quarreling, was one of the things we liked to do. I see this small woman in a baggy T-shirt and a pair of blue jeans, barefoot, a rag tied around her head, shuffling about, pausing to peer at the recipe, spectacles on the end of her nose while she takes a thoughtful pull on her cigarette. Myself meanwhile attempting to keep the work surfaces clear, disposing of peelings, the kitchen *toto*. Nora was only partially attentive while she cooked, but occasionally she paused and, with knife poised aloft, responded. This at least is how I remember it.

Later we would read and listen to music. There was a table in the living room reserved for books. Saturday afternoons we made an expedition to Union Square and came home heavily laden with vegetables and bread and books. Was I wrong to regard this brief period

101

of domesticity as not merely tranquil but as a kind of *flowering?* Intimacy burgeoning, love maturing, all done with the simplest of ingredients, the sharing of ordinary activities with close, unwavering attention paid to the other? Is it any more complicated than that? Need it be?

★　★　★

But occasionally the idyll was disturbed. I came home from the office once in the middle of the day and found her not alone in the apartment. She was at the table, still in her bathrobe, and as I came in she turned toward the door with an expression on her face that I couldn't read. There were papers strewn all over the table. Sitting beside her with a pencil in his hand was my brother.

'Charlie, what are you doing home?' she said.

I ignored her. 'Hello, Walter.'

I once told Nora how my mother would talk to people about her *son*, as though she only had one. She did it in my hearing. I used to say to her, 'What about me, Mom? Aren't I your son too?' I also told her about the time she said to Agnes that anyone could be a psychiatrist, but it took talent to be an artist.

Now here he was in the apartment with her.

'This place almost feels human now,' said Walt. 'Charlie used to keep his shoes in the oven.'

Bluff hearty Walt. I'd felt furious that he would let this happen, that he'd be found with Nora in my apartment while I was supposed to be at work. I assumed she would've told me about his visit, but that wasn't the point. He at least had the grace to leave fairly quickly, having refused the drink I'd felt constrained to offer him. When he'd gone I had asked Nora, coldly, if she'd known he was going to show up.

'Fuck you.'

It came like an arrow. I suppose it was the response I deserved. She was sitting at the table very straight, her eyes strangely bright, a cigarette between her fingers.

I sat down opposite her, rubbed my face and, through sheer force of professional habit, listened to my own words from her point of view. 'All right, you would've told me.'

'Not good enough, Charlie.'

I saw then how pale she was. With shock, I supposed. I pushed myself up out of the chair.

'Don't come near me.'

'Look, can't you just forget I said it?'

'You are so fucking clumsy.'

This was excessive. With rising passion she demanded to know by what right I accused her of lying, what justification could I possibly have for thinking she was — what, seeing Walt behind my back? There was more in this vein. She stormed around the room with fists balled, dramatic gestures appearing, the head lifting to the ceiling — ridiculous, completely out of control. I hate to be called clumsy. I'm not a clumsy man, not physically, not psychologically, but of course it didn't matter who was right or wrong. There *was* no right or wrong, only the reality of her emotion. With an effort of self-control I set aside my own anger, my own *ego*, and told her, without rancor, when she paused for breath, that I was genuinely sorry that what I'd said had caused her pain because that was the last thing in the world I wanted to happen, and that I loved her.

Love. We never talked about love. A moment before she had been unrecognizable, gripped by a rage of such spiraling intensity that she'd become almost ugly. Somehow the idea of love tripped the circuit. Deflated, she sank onto a chair and, with her head bowed, put her hands to her face and quietly wept.

'Here, babe, take this.'

She glanced up and I gave her a clean handkerchief.

She wiped her eyes. 'Charlie, you do get it?' She was determined to make her point, but the storm had passed.

'Forgive me.'

I am a proud man but I am not a slave to my pride. Again, this wasn't about right and wrong. She understood what I'd done, that I'd resolved the situation when I might have made it worse. I stroked her head and led her into the bedroom. A small smile appeared. I saw the little teeth between the red lips, the little pink tongue. How white her skin was. She sat on the bed limp as a rag doll and allowed me to undress her. Caresses were involved, then kisses, and when I had her naked on the bed I flung off my own clothes and joined her there.

Later, she lay with her head on my chest.

'Charlie,' she said, 'it's not that I want to know every last little thing about you because I don't. But you must have a little generosity. You can't just assume the worst of me.'

We grow older, and still we screw up when it comes to generosity. I apologized again. She was eager now to be mollified. We hated to be estranged. Freud once said that signs of conflict are signs of life, but we had life enough without that.

★ ★ ★

This took place on a Friday afternoon and we had the weekend to recuperate, a weekend of pleasure as it turned out, the glimpse of schism serving only to draw us more closely together. I remember the Sunday morning. Still in our bathrobes, we were having bagels, eggs, the works. She was reading the *Times*, her hair uncombed and glasses perched on the tip of her nose. She made some remark, then squinted over the top of her lenses like a bird, a little, delicate, crested American finch. There had been much sex over the weekend. We were both soft, fond, tender. Sore. It occurred to me that it was almost worth having fights if they brought in their wake tranquillity of this high order. I killed the thought at once. I knew what it looked like when she was angry; I'd seen how her anger fed on itself, as though recognition of it aroused further indignation, further rage, thus compounding the original provocation. Then there was no reasoning with her, and to fight back was a mistake. She had spoken to me only obliquely about the arguments she'd had with her ex-husband. I could now understand why the breakdown of that marriage had been so acrimonious.

★   ★   ★

We decided to eat out.

'Where would you like to go?' I said.

'Oh, Sulfur, why not?'

'Why not.'

I put on the suit I'd worn the first time we met, at Walt's dinner party. We cabbed it downtown. We were met at the door by Audrey. It was a warm evening in June and Nora was wearing her simple black dress, arms and shoulders bare, legs bare, and as Audrey led us across the busy room all eyes were upon her, or they should have been. She slid into the banquette as Audrey, with a quick, conspiratorial glance in my direction, gave us menus, the wine list, wished us bon appétit and left.

She was radiant. Her eyes were shining. She gazed at me fondly and reached across the table for my hand. We were both feeling silly with love.

'Hi, babe.'

'Hi, Charlie.'

It was as though all the late unpleasantness had never occurred. The talk meandered as it often did, two lovers nattering across a table, and at some point, for some reason, I mentioned the music I wished to be played at my funeral.

'Oh, don't!' she cried. 'No, really. Don't. It's such bad luck to talk about your own funeral. My father used to talk about his funeral like that, then when he was ill, near the end, he never talked about death at all.'

It was the first time she'd mentioned her father to me, and I couldn't let it pass. I asked her why.

'Too many bad associations. Let's not talk about it.'

Our first course had come and gone. Her steak arrived with a bowl of fries. I was having the grilled tuna and a side of haricots verts. A second bottle of wine was presented, tasted, accepted, poured. She brought up our recent row.

'I'm sorry I put you through it, Charlie. What would I do without you?'

'All over now.'

Again her hand was on mine. She lifted her glass and gazed at me over the top of it. I lifted my own glass. There came a moment around nine when they dimmed the lights and the room grew more intimate. I told her that men and women once solved their problems without people like me. The invention of psychiatry is a relatively late development in human history, I said. Like all good things it came with the rise of the bourgeoisie.

'There's an argument,' I said, 'that psychiatry's overrated. People become dependent on us. They believe nothing has any value unless you pay for it, good advice included.'

'You'll talk yourself out of a job.'

'There's always the tough cases.'

'You're not still angry with Walter, are you? He's been very sweet to me.'

I was aware of a structure in my mind collapsing in slow motion; a psychological implosion, the disappearance of a body of suspicion I'd erected around Nora and my brother. It was oddly liberating, like a darkness lifting. My distrust of Walter was deep-rooted.

'You do have a lot of anger in you, Charlie, and it's really very obvious why.'

'It is?'

'Of course it is. Absorbing all that pain every day. Listening to those ghastly stories.'

In the gloom of the restaurant, each of us leaning forward across the table, we might have been alone in a confessional. Dominant among my various sensations was lust, but I was also keenly interested in the conversation. A little later she suggested we get the check. Normally she'd have ordered a grappa, coffee, spun the night out until she was properly lit. Not this night. Outside the restaurant I kissed her. She was small and pale and gorgeous.

'Shall we just go home, Charlie?'

We took a cab. We came up to the apartment and once inside I poured her a glass of wine and myself a small brandy. We settled down on the sofa. She seemed in no hurry to get to the bedroom and neither was I. There was no tension, no current of unspoken discord that I was aware of. Perhaps a subtle aura of erotic anticipation. She'd kicked off her shoes and there they were on the rug, tiny black suede pumps with chunky heels, the one standing upright, the other nearby lying on its side and their owner, also tiny, sprawled across my lap, one hand hanging over the side of the sofa and the other toying with my shirt buttons. I'd turned on the lamp on the far side of the room. She yawned. The end of a perfect day.

$\star$ $\quad$ $\star$ $\quad$ $\star$

Some hours later she had a nightmare. It was bad. She didn't know where she was, or who I was. It began with a scream, that's what woke me up, and I found her sitting in the bed making violent, stabbing motions with both hands and sobbing with terror. I tried to take her in my arms, but she resisted with all her strength.

'Don't touch me!' she shouted.

I'd seen hysteria like this before, though

not for many years. I tried to restrain her and still she resisted, the stabbing motions now directed at my face and body, and no small number landing with some force until at last I seized her arms and held them to her sides. She was throwing her head from side to side and trying to get out of the bed.

'You're hurting me, let me *go*!'

There was nothing to do but hold on to her until she was exhausted. At last she slumped sobbing in the bed. It was almost over. She lifted her face and stared at me as I held her wrists, murmuring to her in a low voice, saying her name, my own name, telling her where she was. As I held her she grew sleepy and only when the dream began to properly subside was I able to release her wrists. She lay down in the fetal position and at once fell asleep.

Silence.

I rose from the bed and covered her, then sat on the chair by the door and watched her sleep. My thoughts drifted. I remembered the period in my childhood when I'd been awoken every night by a bad dream, and I imagined my mother sitting in my bedroom, watching me as I was watching Nora. It was the dream of my father putting a gun to my head in a dark room and saying he was going to kill me. Mom would come in and comfort me. They were the only times I remember any real warmth and intimacy between us.

The next day Nora's memory of the night was vague. Her struggle with me in the bed had been absorbed into the dream, and the dream had sunk back into her unconscious. She didn't believe what I was telling her in the morning until I opened my shirt and showed her the bruises. She was horrified. She knew she'd been fighting with somebody in her dream, but had no idea it was me.

'Charlie, this is awful.'

'You want to see someone?'

It seemed a reasonable suggestion.

'Oh no! No, don't send me to some stranger! Please don't do that!'

The terror in her face then was not unlike what I'd seen in the night. I told her that no, I'd never send her to some stranger.

8

I was still seeing Agnes during this period and had kept her abreast of developments in my relationship with Nora. She remained opaque with regard to her own relationship, but I felt no such imperative. Usually we'd find an hour in the middle of the day and meet in a small hotel off Third Avenue that we could both reach easily from our places of work, Agnes being at the time a lecturer at Hunter College. She took a keen interest in Nora, and after sex she would question me closely about her. She expressed no jealousy, no hostility toward her that I could detect. I didn't mention the nightmare, though I did tell her about my renunciation of the unconscious on Sundays.

'God, Charlie, I wish you'd tried that with me.'

I was naked, postcoital, stretched out on the bed, my penis damp and flaccid on my thigh. She stood in a bathrobe looking out the window, smoking. She glanced at her watch. We had twenty minutes before we needed to shower and get out of there.

'Was it a problem?' I said.

'You were very earnest. I liked it. You were so political in those days. You're not now.'

'No.'

'What happened? You've become a real cynic.'

Nothing more cynical than a dog, I thought. 'I guess I burned out.'

'I guess you did. What a pity. You're just not all there anymore, Charlie. Something's missing.'

'What?' I said, alarmed.

'Oh, I don't know. Forget it.'

She stubbed out the cigarette and came and lay down beside me. It was a noisy room, the noon-hour midtown traffic loud on the street below, but we liked that. It seemed somehow appropriate for illicit sex in the middle of the day in Manhattan. Something *missing*?

'So what's she like?' she said.

'Can you be more specific?'

'How does she sleep? What's it like, the sleeping together? Not the sex, the sleeping together.'

I hesitated. Why had she asked me that? Agnes at times displayed what I can only call a scalpel-like ability to penetrate other minds, other lives. It was uncanny. Nora slept badly. Even before the nightmare, several times she'd woken me with her thrashing around in the sheets, legs restless as though in her dreams she were running, and small cries and whimpers — there had been a few disturbed nights like this, but when I'd spoken to her in the morning she had no memory of it and no dreams to report.

'Charlie, it's a new bed, it takes me a while to settle down. I didn't keep you awake, did I?'

I told her no, she didn't keep me awake, but it wasn't true. Once woken I do not find it easy to get back to sleep. In the darkness, in the relative silence of the city late at night, anxiety steals in like a wolf. Glimpsing weakness of spirit it circles for the kill, and I would struggle to drive it off but fail, and then I had to go sit in the kitchen and read yesterday's paper until sleep again became possible. This could take an hour, sometimes two. So yes, it was a problem, Nora's disturbed sleep. And she had odd little phobias.

'Charlie, the lights on the ceiling — I hate them. Can't you get someone to move the blinds? You should just replace them, they don't fit the window.'

I was fond of the patterns of light on my ceiling at night, and told her so. She said she'd try to like them too, though I could see they continued to trouble her. I was reluctant to tell Agnes any more but she kept at me.

'It's years since you had somebody in your bed all night. It must be strange.'

'Agnes, I don't ask what goes on in your bedroom.'

'You better not.'

I never asked her about Leon anymore. I went into the bathroom to shower. How well we knew each other. When I'd first suggested we go to a hotel rather than the apartment, she'd figured out the reason at once.

'So you're seeing someone,' she said.

Then, when we met there, she said she could tell it was serious. We hadn't even got our clothes off!

'Why do you think it's serious?'

I was genuinely interested. I often thought Agnes would have made a better psychiatrist than me. She'd turned with a wry cheerful smile, her hands behind her back as she undid her bra, a black lacy affair she knew I liked.

'It may be the loneliness. It's not there anymore. You used to carry it around like a sack of stones.'

'And I don't now?'

She sat down on the bed. Then she stood up again and pulled back the bed cover to inspect the sheets. 'So is it serious?'

'It feels serious.'

She looked up at me then, frowning. I held her gaze. There was no point in trying to conceal it.

'And she's living with you?'

'Yes.'

There was perhaps the faintest flinch, but I might have imagined it. She smoothed the bottom sheet with her palm and lay down with her hands behind her head and one leg crooked at the knee. She was a long pale bony creature in black underwear.

'She have a job?'

'She does research for an art historian.'

I suspect she might have preferred a salesgirl in Bloomingdale's, or a flight attendant. 'Are you angry?'

'No, god knows you've been on your own long enough. I thought you'd get hitched years ago.'

Afterward we must have fallen asleep because when I opened my eyes and remembered where I was, and then looked at my watch, it was nearly one o'clock. Agnes stirred beside me. I sat up.

'It's almost one,' I said.

'Christ.'

But she didn't rush. She ran her fingernails down my spine. 'That was very nice, Charlie,' she said.

At times I did feel some discomfort about

my affair with Agnes, and was aware that I was rationalizing it, telling myself that it didn't really count. Not an argument that Nora would buy — in her eyes, of course, Agnes would be the worst possible rival, far more dangerous than some casual stranger — but in my eyes, and in Agnes's eyes, in the eyes, that is, of the perpetrators of this occasional minor transgression, this flimsy infidelity, it didn't really count. Agnes certainly didn't seem to consider it a matter of any great significance, remarking as we got dressed one time that it was like going to bed with an old shoe.

'An old *shoe?*'

'You know what I mean, Charlie. Comfortable and familiar.'

Never a suggestion from her as to when we would meet again, or that very much had happened at all, in fact, other than the pleasuring of an old shoe. At the door, before we parted, she took my face in her hands and peered at me, frowning, with a small smile that was almost maternal in its tenderness, yet somehow more complicated than that.

'You feel better, Charlie?'

Her concern affected me. I was unprepared for the emotion it aroused.

'Go home and look after that woman,' she said.

* * *

A few nights later Nora again cried out in her sleep and woke us both. I switched on the bedside light. She was sitting upright with her fist pressed to her mouth, staring straight at the end of the bed as though somebody was there.

'What is it?' I whispered.

She was trembling. I touched her arm and she reacted as if she'd had an electric shock, more a spasm than a recoil. She turned to me, her face alive with horror. With a kind of muted wail she reached for me, and I held her. She shuddered in my arms. I rocked her gently, murmuring that it was all right now, whatever had happened was a dream, she was safe now.

'Oh Jesus, that was bad,' she whispered.

'Tell me.'

'I want a cigarette.'

We sat in the kitchen and I made a pot of tea and she smoked. So it was not just random material floating up from the unconscious, I thought. This was the second time. It took some persuading to get her to talk.

'It's not that interesting, Charlie, I'm sure your patients bring you much better stuff.'

'Just tell me,' I said.

I glanced at the clock over the stove. It was after two. The city was quiet except for a distant siren. Her fingers were playing with the cigarette lighter, turning it end on end on the kitchen counter. Eyes staring out of the window, where south of us the twin towers were cliffs of blackness against the pale glow of the sky, narrow rectangular smears of light scattered across them. There was moonlight on the river.

'Someone was following me.'

Standard stuff of nightmare.

'Go on.'

'But that's it!'

'Who's following you?'

She shook her head. I asked her if she didn't know or if she couldn't say.

'Is it a man? Is he threatening you?'

She became thoughtful. She wanted to remember. This was good.

'And there's something else,' she said, 'a sound, but it's kind of negative, like the opposite of wind — '

I saw her suddenly stiffen. I took her hand. She was tense and cold. She was wearing only a T-shirt and pajama bottoms. I asked her if she wanted her bathrobe. She did, so I got it for her. When I came back she had relaxed a little. I helped her slip into the robe. She was still shivering.

'Drink your tea.'

'I've ruined your night. But that's all I can remember.'

'And you've never had it before?'

She shook her head. She didn't think so. She wasn't sure.

'You could hear something like the opposite of wind. A sucking sound?'

'There's this noise it makes, sort of a rumble and a clatter. Loud. And there's a roaring.'

'Is it day or night?'

'Night, I think.'

'Inside or outside?'

Her eyes suddenly filled with tears and again her fist went to her mouth.

'Charlie, can I have a drink?'

'Later. A rumble and a clatter, loud, you said, and a roaring. Like the subway? Were you in the subway, darling? Was someone following you in the subway?'

'And there was laughing.' She turned to me.

'Someone's laughing?' I said.

'And he's coming after me. Oh, Christ.'

'Nora darling, is it *you* laughing?'

She shook her head.

'Who then?'

She shook her head.

'Nora, who's laughing? In your dream, who's laughing?'

She lifted her face. '*My brother!*'

Some weeping then. I didn't want to leave it alone, I wanted her to say it again, but she shook her head. It was enough. After a while I asked if anything had happened to her yesterday that might have triggered the dream, anything she might have seen or read or heard, but she didn't think so. A little later we went back to bed and at once she fell asleep. But I didn't sleep. She'd told me she was an only child. So who was laughing in the nightmare?

★   ★   ★

The next day I had appointments until six. When I got home she was in the kitchen with her head in a recipe book. There was a cigarette burning in the ashtray on the counter and an open bottle of wine. She hadn't turned any of the lights on. I kissed her, and she asked me not to disturb her for a few minutes, she was trying to figure out how to cook this thing. I sat waiting for her. At last she turned the book over and went to the fridge.

'How was your day?' I said.

She grunted.

'You went back to sleep right away.'

'I'm so sorry. Were you exhausted?'

It was said distractedly. She was intent on assembling her ingredients, onions and tomatoes and such. She pushed her hair behind her ears.

'Did you think any more about your dream?'

'I can't deal with that now. Would you pour me some wine? And hand me down the oil. How spicy do you want it?'

'I don't care.'

'We'll have it spicy. I wish you'd fix this drawer.'

She wasn't just irritable, she was avoiding me. It was because of the nightmare. She wasn't going to talk about it. She wanted it back where it belonged, down in the dark. A little later she complained about my very real inadequacy as a handyman. I suggested that since she was in the apartment all day she could talk to the super. If he wouldn't fix the drawer, he'd know someone who could.

'I can't do that,' she said. 'It's not my apartment and anyway, he gives me the creeps. That's the man's job. I do the cooking, I do the washing — '

I lifted my hands, I acquiesced. I knew better than to let a question of mere housework provoke an argument. I told her I'd find somebody. I went to embrace her, but she wasn't having any of that.

'Leave me alone, Charlie, can't you see I'm not in the mood? I thought you were the fucking shrink.'

This last was too much. Irritability I could tolerate, but this was overt hostility and I'd done nothing to provoke it. I sat down on a kitchen stool and stared at my hands. How to deal with it without infuriating her further? I assumed that by helping her in the night, by making her talk about her nightmare, I'd seen something she wanted to conceal from me, or more probably from herself, so now she was angry with me. But what had I seen? A dream involving her being followed, at night, and a roaring, rumbling, clattering noise in the background. What was following her, probably in the subway, that was so terrifying that even these few paltry details created enough panic that she had to punish me for hearing about them? And of course this sudden appearance of a *brother*, when she'd told me she had no brother —

I detected fear of punishment, therefore guilt. It was possible, I thought, that what she remembered was not an actual event but a memory imposed on it in order to disguise it. It is a familiar ruse of the unconscious, to create a scenario capable of inspiring terror, but which in fact is just a screen, a disguising symptom, beneath which lies the memory of trauma proper. Had Nora been traumatized? I wasn't going to ask her, not then. It was by playing what she'd called the fucking shrink that the unpleasantness had arisen in the first place. I left her to the cooking and took a shower.

There was, of course, another possibility, that the laughing man she was fleeing from was not *her* brother, but *my* brother; and that the guilt stemmed from her failure to flee fast enough.

When I returned to the kitchen she came and put her arms around me.

'You will help me, won't you, Charlie?'

9

You will help me, won't you, Charlie? I had
no appointments the next morning but I was
in my office by nine. The night of the dinner
party at Walt's apartment, I'd heard it then,
the almost imperceptible cry for help. I heard
it but I paid no attention to it, and why?
Desire. Desire accompanied by the almost
imperceptible answering cry from somewhere
in my own psyche: yes, my darling, I will help
you. It is the narcissism of the psychiatrist, or
of this psychiatrist, at least, to play the
indispensable figure of succor and healing.
This is how I appeared to my patients. But it
seemed I'd made that same implicit promise
to my lover. I had made the promise and she
had heard me and now she was telling me it
was time.

It was nothing if not oblique. We did the
daily traffic, talking about ourselves, our
work, other people, food, money and such,
and at the same time another conversation
was beginning to go forward, on my side
renewed sexual suspicion, on hers the
discourse of her needs, which she spoke in a
strange, hushed, foreign tongue addressed not

to me but to a primal absent other with whom her arrangements had been made in early childhood, or so I presumed, probably her father. What was I to do?

Nothing. I wasn't her doctor. I'd refer her to someone. There are good reasons why a doctor must not attempt to treat members of his own family and other intimates, as I had learned at great personal cost. It must not happen again. I had no desire to exhume Nora Chiara's childhood. I had no curiosity, no interest in it at all. When I was working at the psych unit and first became familiar with the posttraumatic disorders, I encountered many horrifying nightmares. I came to recognize them as the expression of memories the mind couldn't process and therefore repressed. With someone laughing in her ears Nora had run from a destructive force she called the opposite of wind, then woke up and for several seconds remained trapped in the emotional climate of the dream. She was left sobbing and shuddering, and clung to me like a child. I didn't take this lightly. I was apprehensive the following night, and for several nights after, as to whether there would be a recurrence.

Then came shattering news. For some weeks I'd been worried about Joe Stein. I was aware that there was trouble at home. He was a disturbed man, and to live with him would have been difficult for any woman. I had met his wife once, soon after the beginning of his therapy, and found her to be a competent, mature individual, quite strong enough in my opinion to help steer this tortured man through his crisis. But it seems there came a day when she decided she'd had enough. He had worn her out and used up what to me had looked like a store of goodwill more than adequate to see them through. What had he done to her? Whatever the immediate cause, Stein found himself deserted in his predicament, and rather than go home to an empty house in the suburbs had spent the night drinking whiskey in his office in the financial district.

In the early morning he had climbed out onto the ledge outside his window. High above the street, between the canyon walls of silent office buildings, he had stood flattened against the stone with the wind picking at his clothes and the sun rising over the eastern shores of Long Island, just starting to touch the masonry of the old downtown skyscrapers. I don't know how long he stood on the ledge. He was six stories up. Then he jumped. The fall would surely have killed him had he not landed on the canopy of a sandwich shop on the ground floor, which broke the fall sufficiently that when he crashed through it and onto the sidewalk below he didn't die, although he did fracture his spine. When I arrived at the Beekman Hospital he was in a coma. They would know more, they told me, when the swelling subsided. I sat by his bedside for an hour. Uppermost in my mind was the question of why he hadn't called me. But at the same time I knew why; it was because he'd concluded he was beyond the reach of psychiatry — *I could offer him no hope.* I couldn't touch his conviction of his own worthlessness, which was of course a function of his guilt at having killed a man.

His wife joined me a little later. She'd come in from Westchester. We left the ward and found the cafeteria.

'I guess I'm supposed to feel bad for walking out on him like I did, but I don't. Nobody could've stayed with him. He didn't want me. He as good as threw me out. I think he'd already made up his mind, don't you?'

'I wish you'd have let me know, Mrs. Stein.'

'I thought you did know. I thought you saw him on Tuesday.'

'He concealed it from me.'

'Well, he didn't conceal it from me!'

She glared at me with damp eyes. She blamed me.

'Go on,' I said.

'I was out of my mind. I couldn't deal with him anymore. Do it then, I told him. If you want to do it so bad, why don't you just go ahead?'

'What did he say?'

'Nothing.'

'Was he angry?'

'Not angry, no. He kind of sat down and put his head in his hands and stared at the floor. First I thought he was going to do it, then I thought no, he can't, it's not in him, this thing's eaten him all up, there's nothing left.'

She was struggling. The tears were starting to come.

'Was there really nothing you could do for him?' she said.

I let this question hang in the air. I sat with my elbow on the Formica table in that bright cafeteria as the early sun came streaming in, my hand covering my mouth.

'Frankly, I didn't expect this,' I said.

She recovered her composure. She tipped her head to one side and flattened out her mouth in an expression of skepticism and weary disdain. Her opinion of my competence required no further elaboration. She was a small, slim brunette of about thirty-five.

'At least he's alive. Some small mercy.'

I said nothing.

'They told me they don't know if he'll walk again.'

'We won't know that for a while,' I said.

'Joe in a wheelchair. My god.'

Suddenly she rose to her feet, her chair scraping backward on the tiled floor. A group of nurses at a table nearby gazed at us with tired sympathy. They must be familiar, I thought, with these early-morning dramas involving the family of some poor soul admitted in the night.

'I have to go,' she said. 'I have kids.'

I rose too and offered her my hand. She gazed at it and then shook it with that same flat, glum expression and walked away. I left the hospital and stood in the cool air on Gold Street, staring up at the arches of the Brooklyn Bridge and feeling like hell. I couldn't face going home. I was a five-minute walk from Fulton Street.

When Agnes answered I could hear through the intercom that I'd woken her, but she buzzed me in anyway. Once there had been no intercom, no buzzer, you shouted for whoever you wanted and the key was tossed down in a sock. She opened the door in her bathrobe, blinking and sleepy. It was years since I'd seen this, her early-morning face.

'Is it Cass?' she said.

131

Cassie and her stepfather were in Florida. 'No, it's not Cass.'

'Oh, good.' She shuffled off toward the kitchen, yawning. 'Come in then, Charlie,' she said. 'It's so early. What are you doing here?'

I followed her into the kitchen and sat down. 'I've just come from the Beekman. I couldn't handle going home.'

She was filling the kettle, still three-parts asleep. 'Someone sick?'

'Stein tried to kill himself.'

Now she turned to face me. Now she woke up. 'Oh my god. How is he?'

'He'll live.'

She sat down. She frowned. I remember thinking, a man would want to know what he'd done.

'I'm sure it wasn't your fault,' she said.

To hear those words, was that why I was here? After Stein's wife had glared at me with her damp eyes, accusing me of not doing enough for her husband — was I here to be *absolved?*

'That's exactly what I'd been telling him.'

'Don't let it all compound, Charlie.'

The kettle boiled. She got up and made coffee. The sun was on the Woolworth Building now and it was already a warm day. I felt the tension begin to drain out of me.

'I shouldn't have woken you. I guess I just needed to hear that.'

She made a grunting sound, as though to say, What are friends for? She poured us each a cup of coffee and put a carton of milk on the table. She sat down. 'How's Nora?'

'She's okay.'

The tone shifted. I was on my guard where a moment before I'd allowed myself to wallow briefly in her sympathy. I closed my eyes. Tears came.

'Oh, Charlie.'

She got up and came around the table and sat on my lap, putting her arms around my neck and her face in my shoulder. I held her tentatively. How well I knew the warm body beneath the bathrobe and the flimsy cotton nightgown. It was as though we'd just risen from the same bed. As my hold grew firmer she pulled back a little.

'You do make heavy weather, Charlie.'

'Do I?'

What did this mean? I didn't care what it meant, I just didn't want her to get up.

She got up. She stood looking down at me.

'Come back,' I said.

Instead she reached out a hand. 'Come on,' she said quietly. 'Come to bed.'

* * *

133

I sat on the E train computing implications and constructing lies. For reasons I was too tired to work out, it seemed much worse to have gone to Agnes for consolation than for sex. But I'm a pragmatic man, and there was no undoing what had occurred. It couldn't be more simple, I thought. It will not happen again; no boat will be rocked, no house will fall down. All that was required of me was to look as if I'd spent a number of hours at the bedside of a failed suicide. But I disliked the prospect; it is always shabby to deceive even if in doing so you spare the other pain. In the event I was excused even that piece of business: Nora was in the library all day.

I arrived home that afternoon after my last appointment to find her in the apartment. She was eager to hear about Stein; she, too, had been woken when the call came early that morning. I was aware that I was sustaining my campaign of rationalization, my conviction that this thing I had with Agnes *didn't really count*; and this being so, the point, the only point, was to protect Nora's peace of mind. But no suspicion was even hinted at.

We went out for dinner. We had lobster in the Chelsea Hotel, Nora drank a bottle of wine and we walked home along Twenty-third Street. As I prepared for bed I stared in the bathroom mirror. About the man behind the face I felt neutral. I didn't dislike him but I didn't particularly like him either. There he was, Charlie Weir, dog. That night the nightmare came back.

★ ★ ★

I had an idea what to expect now. She would want to smoke a couple of cigarettes while she calmed down. Then she'd want a drink. She wouldn't want to talk about it. She would then fall deeply asleep and not wake again until morning. And this was what happened. The next day she behaved as though nothing was wrong. We were supposed to be having dinner with Walt and Lucia but she asked me to call Walt and make some excuse. I did so.

'Thanks, Charlie.'

'Let me ask you a question.'

We were in the living room. The sky was still light to the west. She was looking at a magazine. Her hair was pushed up on top of her head in a messy clump, a clip holding it in place.

She looked at me over the top of her reading glasses. She was wary. 'Okay.'

'You want to see someone? You want me to refer you to someone?'

Surely there was cause for concern. She couldn't say I was overreacting.

'Let me think about it.'

She spoke quietly, and I detected no defensiveness. Certainly no anger.

'All right.'

It took her longer this time to regain her equilibrium. I watched her closely. The decision to seek help must come from her alone and without pressure from me. Three or four days later she talked about it. We were reading in bed, and I was about to turn out the light.

'Do I have to see someone?' she said suddenly.

'I think you do.'

'Why?'

'It's happened three times now.'

'Listen, you live in New York, you have bad dreams, it's the city. It's a war zone, Charlie, you have to be a warrior to live here.' She lay back and stared at the ceiling. Then she sat up again. 'Can't I just see you? I mean, if it happens again, couldn't you just talk me through it? I really don't want to go into therapy just for a couple of bad dreams.'

I told her I couldn't treat her. It was out of the question.

She spoke without thinking. 'You treated Agnes's brother.'

'Exactly.'

'And you have bad dreams too.'

136

'Not like you.'

We were silent for a while. Her mood troubled me. It suggested she was in denial about what I suspected might be the symptoms of posttraumatic stress. The nightmares. The heavy drinking. A kind of mental absence at times, a dissociation of affect that occurred even during sex.

'Okay. Turn the light out.'

She was soon asleep. But I lay there in the darkness, irritated that she was so casual about this, and that she could be careless enough to bring up Danny. *You treated Agnes's brother* — had she no idea of the effect that would have on me? She didn't know because I hadn't told her, but my own bad dreams, which produced far fewer theatrical effects than hers, invariably involved Danny. I was the one who found the body.

★ ★ ★

Joe Stein woke up from his coma and spent several days heavily sedated. I visited him during this period. He lifted a hand off the blanket. He had a tube in his mouth. In his doped eyes I detected an expression of wry resignation. Even at the toughest times in his therapy Stein's sense of humor would flicker to life. He was always able to detach himself from his anguish, if only briefly.

'You must be pretty worried,' I said.

He lifted his eyebrows. I imagined if he could speak he would have said, Are you kidding me?

'You know there's every chance you'll walk again.'

He nodded. I believed he needed to hear this as often as possible. Whatever he'd been feeling when he was out on that ledge, he didn't feel it now. Apparently he'd got through an entire bottle of scotch. Something occurred to me.

'I wonder if you really did jump.'

He gazed blankly at me.

'Could it be you just *slipped?*'

I spent twenty minutes with him. I told him I'd seen his wife, and that it was my impression she'd be there for him when he got out of here. He lifted his eyebrows at this. He seemed glad of the visit. I said I'd be back to see him soon.

It was just after six when I left the hospital. It was a warm clear evening with just a breath of a breeze off the East River. Again it occurred to me to go to Fulton Street, but I stepped down hard on that idea. I was going home.

Home. For a second I recoiled from the idea that the apartment on Twenty-third

Street was home anymore. It seemed instead a sort of clinic, housing one patient. All at once I felt a flare of resentment toward Nora, the fact that she was sick and had somehow become my responsibility, and this in spite of my repeated insistence that I couldn't treat her, that she wasn't my patient and never could be. It was rush hour, and the E train was crowded and hot. I was tightly packed among a group of commuters who looked as irritable as I felt. Were they all going home to a neurotic woman?

I would like to say she greeted me with warm solicitude, and that the last of my tension and anger dissipated within minutes of my walking through the door. It did not. She was in a foul mood. By now I understood that Nora had been unable, or refused, rather, to learn a single, simple, indispensable principle of human relations, which is that you don't take out your anger on those closest to you *unless* they're directly responsible for it. It was of course another aspect of the pathology. But I didn't think this was the time to tell her so.

'You haven't spoken to the super, have you?' she said. She was avoiding my eyes and clattering about the kitchen, making too much noise with pots and pans. 'This fucking drawer, will it never get fixed?'

139

She wrenched the troublesome drawer with both hands and so violently that I fully expected it to come clear out of the unit and spill cutlery all over the kitchen floor. This was probably what she wanted, an explosion of stainless steel on the tiles.

'What's wrong?' I said.

Oh, and now the quick sideways baleful glance, eyes hot with rage, and it occurred to me that she sensed I had betrayed her but could neither account for the feeling nor even precisely define it, and instead displaced it onto a kitchen drawer.

'You tell me, Charlie. I won't be treated like this. I don't see why I should live here and be treated like this.'

'Like what?'

I was sitting on a kitchen stool staring at my hands, which were splayed flat on the countertop.

'You're so fucking *cold*.'

She stood on the other side of the counter with her back against the stove staring at me. She was clutching a metal spatula as though to defend herself. The tears came. I did not go to her at once.

'You see?' she cried. 'You're made of *ice*!'

With a large, weary sigh I pushed the stool back and got to my feet.

'No! No. Too late, Charlie. I don't want

comforting. You have to love me.'

'I do love you.'

She had turned her back on me. She made no pretense of activity at the stove, just gave me her back with her shoulders heaving slightly. I groped for the means of resolving the situation. It was immaterial who was right or wrong here; the only fact of any importance was her pain.

'Nora, I do love you. Why do you think I don't?'

'You never show it anymore.'

Still her back was to me, but the voltage was down.

'You think so?'

She put her hands on the stove and leaned over with her head bowed. She was sobbing. I wanted to be touched, to be moved, to care, but I couldn't seem to.

'I can't stay here,' she muttered.

Then something did move. There was a spark of some kind, something, at least — probably pity, though it didn't much matter what it was — and I went to her and turned her toward me. She allowed herself to be embraced and held. After a few moments she pulled free and left the kitchen. Hearing the bathroom door close, I went to the other end of the room and leaned against the window frame and gazed out toward the river. The last light was fading from the sky over Jersey, and there was a rusty smear of a sunset.

I felt empty. It was a state of mind with which I was familiar but hadn't experienced in a while. I understood it as a mechanism of denial, which closed off emotion and sensation so as to protect me from being flooded. It was a flaw in my psyche for which I compensated by treating neurotic women for a living, and it was connected to Danny. After his suicide, and in the knowledge that I was responsible for it, I had been prone to states of emotional flatness and inertia, a sort of inner deadness. There'd been other symptoms too, more intrusive symptoms, for instance the dreams about him, what he'd looked like when I found him. I'd never had them seen to and I suppose I should have. This was why my marriage had collapsed with such suddenness, and why I'd been an emotional isolate for the past seven years. It was what I think Agnes meant when she said I had something missing. And now it was happening again.

It is truly demoralizing to feel yourself powerless to prevent the repetition of a pattern of behavior that you recognize as productive only of suffering. I had helped many distressed men and women, more often women, to confront and eventually disrupt such patterns of compulsive behavior; but apparently I couldn't do the same for myself.

Nora and I later made some sort of peace, both of us exhausted by what had occurred and by the stresses underlying its occurrence. The next day, after my last appointment, I walked east to Lexington Avenue to catch the downtown train. On impulse, I don't know why, I got off at Astor Place and walked up Fourth Avenue to Union Square and sat on a bench under a tree. It was a dank, humid day with low clouds. There was an ugly feel to the city. It was suddenly the hot, unpleasant season in New York, and there had been a murder in Washington Heights that sounded like an eerie echo of Son of Sam, who'd terrorized us two summers back. I had the impression that my life had become an exercise in pointless circularity.

★   ★   ★

There was now no doubt that Nora and I were in a state of crisis, and that if our relationship were to be saved it would have to be me who did the saving. Knowing this, why then did I continue to see Agnes? In retrospect it seems clear that I intended things with Nora to break down, that I

143

wanted her to leave me but was unable to act on that wish because I recognized her fragility and suspected how deeply she was damaged. I certainly didn't want to be the agent of her breakdown. So I was providing asylum, protecting her, and from what? From myself. I had in fact become her doctor without intending to, and as her doctor I was shielding her from the man to whom she'd given her love but who'd grown weary of her and wished now to push her out. I was a divided man, doctor and lover, each contending with the other over the unstable psyche of Nora Chiara. For a number of days the two opposing impulses existed in a state of near-perfect equilibrium, but I was not so much a body at rest as a body in paralysis.

We coexisted in a state of mutual detachment. We were largely silent, coolly polite to each other, but each for our own reasons unwilling to initiate the argument we knew would involve saying things that could never be unsaid. For both of us this awful icy silence was preferable to an apocalyptic row after which life would never be the same. There is a conservative element in most relationships and it tolerates much that is outrageous, or that later comes to be seen as such.

Nora and I were neither of us ready for upheaval. She was stronger than I expected. She'd steeled herself to what she saw as my iceman nature and was prepared — this seemed her unspoken position — to sustain the status quo until it could be sustained no longer, which would be a time of her choosing. I had resumed visiting Agnes, coming downtown in the middle of the day when Cassie was at school. I told her what was happening at home.

'You don't need that, Charlie,' she said. 'Not with everything else you have to contend with.'

10

I'd often thought that Agnes would have made a much better psychiatrist than me. As a teacher of sociology her interest lay in what I thought of as the dramaturgical model of social life: all human interaction as performance, each one of us an actor, the self a sort of colloquium. I remember how we used to quarrel over the concept of emotion, about which she expressed real skepticism. It was our most divisive issue.

I trusted Agnes but she didn't understand Nora's pathology. All that *anger!* — what the hell was I supposed to do about her? She wouldn't go into therapy, and *I* certainly wasn't going to sort out her childhood for her. So what sort of future could we contemplate? The next time I saw Agnes I told her all this. We were in our midtown hotel, getting undressed. She understood then that the situation was more complicated than she'd realized. I told her I thought that maybe I should treat Nora after all. It wasn't so very complicated.

She was horrified. 'Are you out of your

mind? You tried to treat Danny, had you forgotten?'

It was hard to hear this. I told her I was young then, and inexperienced. I wouldn't make the same mistake again. I said I thought it would be a pretty straightforward course of therapy, just tidy her up —

Agnes was brisk in her response. 'Tidy her *up*? Forget about that! Just cut her loose, Charlie. Let her go.'

Cut her loose. Let her go. She was right. We had no future. She found me cold and I found her needy, moody and short-tempered. I also thought she was untrustworthy; I was still deeply suspicious of her relationship with my brother. So, yes, cut her loose. At the same time she was still intensely sexually attractive to me, and some part of it sprang from her wildly volatile nature. The problem was that she needed help, but that Charlie Weir was the last person on earth to provide it. *Unless* — and this only occurred to me when I was on my way back to the office — *unless* she agreed to an intensive, fixed-limit, goal-directed program of no more than twelve sessions over a period of six weeks.

★ ★ ★

I had only one appointment that afternoon, a patient I thought of as *My Abused Woman*. Her name was Elaine Smith. Elly. She was a very attractive young attorney in the D.A.'s office who showed all the signs of having suffered, as a child, sustained sexual abuse at the hands of her father. He was dead now. He had been a distinguished financier in the city. Like Nora, Elly was still resisting the pressure of her memories, and growing panicked as she began to realize that resistance was futile. She had become angry that afternoon and acted out. She had cursed me, then strutted around my office in a fine state of outrage. She'd tossed her hair and slapped at her thigh with a rolled-up copy of the *New York Times*. Then she bluntly propositioned me, suggesting that the therapy would go a great deal more smoothly if we had sex just once. I'd encountered this before. My quiet refusal seemed only to inflame her rage and then she collapsed, weeping, onto the chesterfield.

It had been a strenuous hour, but an important hour. I made sure she understood this before I let her go. I waved aside her tearful apologies and assured her she'd done good work and that this would soon be apparent to her.

When she'd gone I took off my jacket and stretched out on the chesterfield myself, my hands behind my head. There were a number of reasons why I didn't believe Nora had been abused as Elly had, foremost among them her uncomplicated attitude toward sex. But the two women did share a strong antagonism to their fathers, which accounted for the anger they both directed at me: paternal transference of the most primitive kind. The difference between them, of course, was the fact that I was seeing Elly as a *patient*; and thinking this, I felt the familiar anger began to stir. But now I had a specific proposal for Nora. If she agreed to it then we could perhaps put this destructive behavior behind us for good.

★   ★   ★

That night we were going out to dinner with Walt and Lucia, who were shortly to leave for Italy, and I had only a few minutes to tell her about my idea. She was in the bathroom applying her makeup. She showed mild interest but said we should talk about it tomorrow. She had to get tarted up, she said, and it was already after seven. She seemed more concerned about her lipstick than her mental health.

We were eating at Sulfur, which was busy. Audrey took us to a table in the back of the room. Nora was in a subdued mood but Walt was in good spirits and at once ordered a gin martini.

'And one for me,' I said.

The women would also have martinis, and Walt was pleased about this. Watching him, I remembered the pleasure my mother used to take in seeing her favorite son enjoying himself, and recalled those special occasions, usually a birthday — this would be after Fred left us — when she took us out to a good restaurant for dinner. Walt loved to eat in restaurants even then, though I was far less at ease with waiters looming over me demanding to know what I wanted. Mom would gaze at me, the waiter standing impassively with pad and lifted pencil, Walt's eyes meanwhile darting about the busy room.

'Come on, Charlie, you must make up your mind.'

'Can I have a steak, please?'

'You always have steak,' said Walt.

'Are you sure?' Mom said.

'No. Yes.'

Flustered, furious, I would then have to decide how I wanted it cooked. But Walt knew that as his mother's guest he had to sing for his supper, and he'd been doing it ever since, even when the table was his own. Nothing had changed. We sat there at Sulfur, the women laughing as he grew warm telling some story, and I nodded and sipped my martini and kept an eye on Nora.

It was late in the meal that it happened. Lucia had gone to the washroom, and Nora was telling Walter about her work. It wasn't going well. Writing was hell, she said.

'Charlie can help, surely,' said Walt.

I was for a moment unsure what he was saying, whether the spirit of the remark — was I not the man who helped people who were stuck in hell? — was benign or the reverse. It hardly mattered. What did matter was Nora's answer.

'Charlie doesn't even know what I'm doing,' she said.

She turned toward me. I hadn't really been following the conversation.

'What?'

'I think if I left him he wouldn't even notice.'

'I'm sure he'd *notice*,' said Walt.

'After a week.'

'Now this isn't very useful,' I said.

Walt was leaning forward, his elbows on the table, looking from one of us to the other. He relished moments like this. But where had it all suddenly come from? Was she drunk?

'I don't think anybody wants to be questioned too closely about their work, do they?' I said. 'Particularly writers. Artists, maybe.'

Walt did not rise to this. He could have, but he chose not to. He wanted to hear more of Nora's bile, delighted to listen to a woman's anger not for once directed at himself.

'Have you tried?' she said.

'I think I have.'

My hands were folded on the table. My gaze was calm, steady, sober. I was glad only Walt was here. I realized she was very angry. She wouldn't look at me, her hands were restless and there was a sort of simmering menace that made me apprehensive. She was unpredictable in this state. She was also, curiously, very beautiful. It was passion that made her so.

'Do you ever think about me, Charlie, if I'm not in the room?'

'Do we need to do this here, darling?'

'Walt knows what you are. Tell him, Walt.'

Walt opened his hands as though to show he had no concealed blades, this a sure sign he was about to tell a lie.

'So tell me, Walter,' I said.

His eyes drifted across the room. He wanted Lucia to come back and defuse this suddenly dangerous situation.

'Then I'll tell him,' said Nora.

'Tell me what?'

They must be having an affair. How else do men and women come to such intimacies as this, I mean Walt's candid opinion of me, whatever it was, little though I cared?

'He thinks you're not truly alive.'

Not truly *alive*! What a shit. What a complete and utter shit. 'Thanks, Walter. And when did he share this penetrating aperçu with you?'

'I was exaggerating,' said Walt. 'But see, now you employ sarcasm, Charlie, you employ irony. You're just so damn cerebral all the time.'

That was enough. I rose to my feet.

'Oh, sit down and don't be an asshole,' said Nora. 'We're only talking.'

She was drunk. I threw my napkin on the table. I wanted to fling a glass of wine in her face, in his face, in somebody's face. Lucia appeared.

'What's going on?' she said as she sat down.

'Good night,' I said.

I walked south, heading for Fulton Street, for Agnes, driven by blind instinct, but I didn't get that far. I thought better of it. I took a cab home. I took a sleeping pill. In the morning I left the apartment before Nora was awake.

When I got home that evening she'd moved out. There was a brief typewritten note: *Charlie, it's not working. I've gone to Audrey's. N.*

★   ★   ★

Well, relief, at first. But not for long. More bad news: Dr. Sam Pike died. I heard about it at home. Massive coronary, I might have predicted it. I did predict it, in fact, we all did, all of us who knew that blustering, fallible, tenderhearted man. The greatest psychiatrist I ever knew, my teacher, my mentor and my friend. This was a man who could not only understand but also empathize, *identify* with any and every species of experience known to man. I once asked him if he could empathize with a necrophiliac.

'I have,' he said.

This was during my wilderness years, after I left Agnes. Sam and I worked closely together during that period, and it probably saved me. We collaborated on a book about trauma. We made the world remember — for it had forgotten, yet again — the clinical reality of the posttraumatic disorders. We established diagnostic criteria and constructed therapeutic regimes. We gave special emphasis to the creation of the *trauma story*,

154

the detailed narrative of the emotion, the context and the meaning of trauma. We'd been sitting up late in his office drinking whiskey from paper cups, talking about the effects on the psyche of the commission of extreme transgressive acts like the sexual abuse of a child. That's when I'd asked him if he could empathize with a necrophiliac.

'All right,' I said, 'but what about an *eater* of the dead?'

'That too. You knew him.'

A clear night in late summer, the window open, the distant hooting of a vessel in the harbor. All the other usual night sounds of New York City. We were both exhausted. I waited for him to say more. Suddenly he looked up, light in his eye and his lip wet. Significant movement in that baggy mind of his.

'You know who I'm talking about.'

'I don't think I do.' He was making no sense.

'You do.'

'Who, Sam? Jesus!'

Then I saw it. Danny, of course. Danny ate the dead.

There was a memorial service in a church on Park Avenue a month or so later, and the number of people who showed up illustrated if nothing else the breadth of Sam's influence.

They came from all over the world, men and women whom he'd trained or treated or whose lives he had somehow touched and never superficially. I had for some years realized the extent to which my status within the psychiatric community reflected my close association with Sam Pike. I knew that our work had had a profound effect on certain areas of psychotherapy, largely the treatment of sexually abused women and children. The day of Sam's memorial I was forcibly reminded that I had come a long way in the profession. My private life was something else again, but my work had not been for nothing.

But I felt the lack. The gnawing sense of my own incompletion. I left the church and walked south. The inescapable fact of emotional failure again. Not truly alive. Already dead, then. Solitude was familiar, solitude was an old shoe, but this new solitude after Nora's departure had an ominous undertone to it that hadn't been there before, like the muffled chiming of a distant bell. I tried to write to her but it proved impossible because I didn't know what I wanted to say, other than that I understood why she'd left me. It was obvious: she was terrified by the prospect of six weeks of intensive psychotherapy. She didn't want to know what was wrong with her. She didn't *want* to remember.

Saying this, however, would be counterproductive. Her denial would only grow more stubborn, more impregnable. So I remained alone. I had my work, yes, but at the end of the day I came home through a dirty, frightened city to an apartment in which the telephone never rang and the mailbox almost never held a message of any importance. There was nothing I wanted to do except sleep, and during the day to escape into the problems of others. I dimly recognized the features of the old depression returning, the depression I'd idly thought of as my inheritance, left me by my mother instead of an apartment. Though there was of course Agnes.

I called her the following Saturday and told her that Nora had left me.

'Oh Charlie, what are we going to do with you?'

She asked me to come to supper as Leon was out of town, and I agreed with some alacrity. I bought a good bottle of wine and got a haircut. I presented myself at Fulton Street at seven sharp and was surprised by my own fierce pleasure at walking into a warm, well-lit apartment with the smell of cooking, and the music of Monk, and a daughter who kissed me, and there was

Agnes, drying her hands on a dish towel, a tall, kindly heron of a woman regarding me warmly and shaking her head.

'Oh, you poor battered man,' she said.

Cassie was full of compassion too, although she had no idea why I deserved it. 'Yes, poor battered Daddy!' she cried.

She flung her arms around me and clung to me for half a minute, pretending to sob, and I had to gently detach her as I couldn't move. One of the reasons I remained so popular with Cass was because I was the Saturday parent. I took her out to lunch, I took her swimming, I took her to the movies. I never had to tell her to finish her homework or tidy her room, I just showed up and asked her what she wanted to do. She was flirtatious with me, affectionate, eager to confirm that I was her real daddy, not like Leon. We talked about her schoolwork, then I asked Agnes how her sister, Maureen, was doing and she said Cassie had seen her more recently than she had.

'She's doing good,' Cassie said. She was sprawled in the armchair with her book. She didn't lower it. She'd lost interest in me now. Her rudeness I found oddly pleasing; it told me I was at home here and she was comfortable with me. Isolated people, those who live alone, are always conscious of their condition in the homes of families. Agnes knew I wanted to talk about Nora and that I wouldn't be able to until Cassie had gone off to her room.

After we'd eaten, Cassie disappeared. I washed the dishes. I noted with irritation the pleasure it gave me to perform this chore. I was aware of something soft in me, something weak, that I should be so pitifully incapable of accepting the fact that I was once more alone. It was my responsibility. I had created it. Why then did I hanker for the treacherous warmth of a shared kitchen, a shared bed? Twice I had known it, twice I had lost it, willfully and deliberately each time. I think I must have stood for a few seconds in front of the sink, unmoving, rigid with complicated displeasure, and Agnes saw it.

'Sit down, Charlie,' she said quietly.

I did as I was told.

'Talk to me.'

She sat there rolling a cigarette, an empty wineglass in front of her, a bowl of grapes on the table. From the back of the apartment, from Cassie's bedroom, came muted pop music.

'I seem to be the only one who was taken by surprise,' I said.

'What are you going to do now?'

Her face lifted to mine. I noticed how the

eyelids had begun to droop at the corners, giving her eyes a slightly hooded look, and that the crosshatched lines beneath them were spreading across her cheekbones. The clefts in her cheeks were grooves now but it was all natural ravage, not the effects of dissipation, just the stuff time does with flesh. All this daily aging and changing, and me not there to observe it. Her hair was still the color of old straw, and no more kempt than when I'd first met her.

'I don't know you anymore,' I said.

'For god's sake, Charlie.'

'I don't know what I'm going to do.'

'You don't want her back?'

I tried to explain the position Nora's illness had put me in, my reluctant agreement that I would treat her, and her then promptly walking out on me. Agnes said nothing. She didn't ask again if in spite of it all I wanted her back.

'You probably thought it was a big mistake from the start,' I said, 'and obviously you were right, but it didn't feel like that.'

'I don't suppose I should have expected — ' She left the thought unfinished.

'What?'

'I shouldn't have expected you to be smarter than anybody else. You've been alone a long time. But you mustn't try to treat her.'

'Do *you* want me back?'

It was reckless of me to ask. It made her angry. I knew it would.

'What is wrong with you, Charlie? Aren't you satisfied with all the damage you've done? How can you be so — '

'So what?'

'So *obtuse.*'

Well, yes, that was the point, wasn't it? I grew suddenly impatient of feeling like, I don't know, a piece of damp lettuce. I said this. She didn't respond.

'I'd better go,' I said.

'Oh, have another drink or something,' she said.

She got up and stood at the window. Then she went back to the sink and ran cold water into the pot she'd boiled the pasta in. I poured myself a little wine. There was still one glass left in the bottle. I grew reckless once more.

'I want you back,' I said.

Instantly there came a kind of sigh from Agnes, part exasperation and part sorrow. Now she'll throw me out for sure, I thought, but she didn't.

'You know what this looks like, don't you, Charlie? Your girlfriend walks out and you run straight back to me. You come here and tell me it's me you want now. That's what it looks like. How am I supposed to feel about that?'

'How *do* you feel about that?'

She was sitting at the table now, gazing straight at me, and she was angry, but not angry like Nora, not destructively angry, not hysterically angry. Seriously annoyed, rather.

She gave a snort of amusement and picked up her napkin. 'You are the end,' she said.

I reflected on it later: you are the end. I should have said, *And you are the beginning*, but what kind of nonsense was that?

'I don't know why I'm so fond of you,' she said.

Now this I took very seriously indeed. This was in the nature of a major development, a breakthrough. I stared at her intently. I remembered how we used to do this long ago, stare into each other's face without blinking.

'But it makes no difference,' she said.

'Why not?'

No answer. Displacement activity. Pour herself a little wine. Push the glass around, slopping the wine from side to side. Cassie's door opened, a blast of sound.

'Mom!'

'Later.'

The door closed, the music muffled once more. I smiled.

'Yeah,' said Agnes.

Where were we? She'd told me it made no difference that she was fond of me. I wanted her very badly and all at once I saw it was possible. Not just possible, inevitable. She'd been waiting for me. Seven years apart, so what. My one other serious relationship in ruins, so what. All the more reason. There was a clear light in my head.

'Calm down, Charlie,' she said.

But the light was still there, and it didn't go out even as she threw back her wine in one swallow and stood up from the table.

'I'm going to bed now. By myself.'

'When can I see you again?'

'Oh, *Charlie*.'

But at the door of the apartment she let me kiss her, and I held her very close for several seconds until she turned away, and with her face averted pushed me out into the corridor and closed the door. A few moments later I was out on the sidewalk in the heat of the night with the traffic stalled and honking on Nassau Street, and I didn't feel merely better than I had in years, I felt like a man who'd just got out of jail.

* * *

That night I dreamed I attended the funeral of Leon O'Connor. It took place at an old indoor swimming pool. Through a set of high glass doors I entered a hall of watery shadows with a vaulted roof where long glass panes, black with dirt, were framed between arching iron ribs. Large-bulbed lamps in broad tin shades were suspended in a line from a traverse beam high above the water, but they couldn't dispel the sepulchral gloom of the place. Birds fluttered high in the obscurity. Dead birds floated in the water. There was a dense crush of firemen and I had to squeeze among them to reach the coffin, where I could just glimpse Agnes and Cassie. They hadn't seen me, and it was important that they know I was here. The firemen made it difficult for me to get through, and as I moved across the damp slippery duck-board I almost lost my footing several times, and had to cling to one or another of them for support. There was a smell of mold and chlorine, also indistinct booming sounds I took to be the words of the service. At last I reached the coffin, but it wasn't a coffin anymore. Now it was a metal gurney, and it wasn't Leon lying on it. It was Danny.

I awoke with a start, sweating, trembling, short of breath; I felt I was suffocating. It was the familiar horror, seeing the body as though for the first time. This is what trauma is. The event is always happening *now*, in the *present*, for the *first time*.

11

Sam Pike and I had been hearing stories of men who went berserk in the war. The vets talked about them in a way that was hard to define precisely. First there was a kind of incredulity, which shaded into dismay, even disapproval, but within a matter of seconds you could hear admiration and then reverence steal into their voices. As though someone who so clearly should have been excluded from the society of men was possessed at the same time of transcendent power capable of arousing awe. These were soldiers who exposed themselves to certain death and survived, at least for a while, who jumped onto the fortifications and blazed away at the enemy and did not fall. Men who'd gone over the edge into sustained outrage and fury, and in that state seemed to the soldiers around them to have assumed an almost godlike status because they were no longer restrained, no longer afraid, careless of their own lives and unrelenting in their aggression. Most men who went berserk were spoken of in the past tense because they didn't survive for long. They behaved as though they were invulnerable, these wild gods who loved killing and showed no mercy and could not die until of course they did die. A number of guys in the group had stories about such soldiers, and it became clear that in certain men exposed to sustained danger in combat a distinct pathology emerged, one of its features being this raging suicidal recklessness. I began to suspect that this had happened to Danny.

He was getting into fights. One time he appeared at the group with a heavy bandage on his hand. Frequently there were cuts and bruises on his face. Another time he limped in, hurting badly from an injury to his foot. There was no point in asking him what had happened. Danny wasn't someone you asked such questions, though I did try to look after the wound on his hand. I told him we could go up to Surgery, where I'd clean it up and give him a new dressing. But no, he was okay. 'Forget about it, Charlie. It's cool.' I told Billy Sullivan I was worried. Did he know what was going on? With the effects of heavy drinking growing ever more apparent, and the various abrasions on him, and the limping and the bandages, he looked like a street person or a bum.

'He loses it,' said Billy, 'he just fucking explodes. You have to get out of there, and fast, man. There's no way of predicting it. He feels like shit afterward.'

'Explodes, what, with rage?'

'Rage, sure. Then he'll just start throwing stuff, bottles, whatever, and when they try to throw him out it's this big bust-up and that's why he comes in looking like a train wreck.'

Billy was a bear of a man. He'd piloted helicopters for a reconnaissance unit in the combat zone and saw his copilot melted by a stream of flame from a shell that hit the chopper but failed to detonate. I remember him telling the story bent forward with his elbows on his knees and his head sunk low. At the end he had lifted his head. His face was the color of ash.

'Should've been me, man,' he said.

So Billy shed some light on what happened to Danny when he was out in the bars. These episodes of explosive rage weren't particularly surprising in a man who for several months had lost any sense of moderation in combat, including concern for his own survival. Danny could not speak of these things, but it was clear to me that he wouldn't heal until he did speak.

One of his few contributions to the group had stuck in my mind.

'I never expected to get home alive,' he said. 'I never wanted to.' There was a silence.

He heaved a sigh, blew out some air. 'Fuck, I never did.'

'Did what, man?'

Danny looked up with a grin. 'Get home alive.'

What a wealth of pathology lay in that admission. It was the first time I'd encountered a man so profoundly alienated from his own humanity that he felt already dead. I decided not to tell Agnes about it, but I did tell Sam Pike. He asked me what I imagined would happen if I asked Danny straight out what he'd done that he found so hard to confront. Was I afraid there'd be violence?

'I think he might stop showing up.'

'And?'

Sam had a swivel chair in his office high in the building, overlooking the East River, and he liked to suddenly swivel away and stare out the window. It allowed him to swing back when he chose to, the effect dramatic.

'I think if I say nothing one day he'll feel secure enough to start talking about it.'

Sam had his back to me. 'So what's the problem?'

'Because that day might never come, and while I wait he's in hell.'

Sam was silent. We stared out across the water at the Long Island City warehouses. It was summertime. The day was still, the drowsy water sparkling in the sunlight. A tugboat came down the river; a police launch headed up. The silence continued, one minute, two. Silence is never innocent in a psychiatrist's office. Sam was waiting.

'He's a very sick guy,' I said. It sounded inadequate even to my ears.

Sam swung back around and lurched forward, his hands coming down flat on the desk. 'For Christ's sake, man, why not just tell him? Tell him you want to know. See if he's got a problem with that.'

'Perhaps.'

'Perhaps,' he snorted.

Sam was my boss, but of course he was much more than that. My idealization of him was a kind of compensation for my own father's inadequacy, so he was a paternal surrogate onto whom I projected frustrated filial needs. We both knew that. When he suggested I confront Danny I questioned the approach I'd been taking up to then, which largely reflected the attitude of the group, the habit of respecting the special status Danny had acquired, which somehow exempted him from having to talk about what had happened before they shipped him home.

I said this to Agnes when I got back to Fulton Street that night. Cassie was a year old then. We were sitting at the table when I told her I thought it might be the moment to push Danny harder. Agnes worried constantly about her brother, and at times I imagined her asking herself why we didn't seem able to help him. I hoped with this suggestion to deflect what I felt to be her unspoken accusation that we were doing nothing for him. But to my surprise she didn't at once warm to the idea. We had finished eating. I rose from the table and gathered the plates, and as she sat rolling a cigarette I watched her from the sink.

'I don't know,' she said. Absently she chewed at her lower lip, something she did when she was anxious. She pushed her hair back from her forehead.

'You think I shouldn't?'

'This is Sam's idea?'

'Mine. I discussed it with him.' A small lie, this, which would come back to haunt me.

'But he thought it was a good idea?'

I nodded.

'I don't know,' she said again.

Her doubt strengthened my resolve. I had always participated in Agnes's tortured deliberations about her brother, and shared her preoccupation with the difference the war had made to him. She seemed unable to forget the man he'd been before he went, and what he was now.

'He's getting worse,' she said.

'I know.'

'He looks terrible.'

'I *know*!'

Nobody doubted that Danny was tough; more than tough, he was indestructible. And although he was abusing his body mightily it showed no sign of breaking down anytime soon. The damage was superficial, the scrapes and gashes he acquired in barroom scuffles, and the puffiness that came with the drinking. He ate solid food and had a rent-controlled apartment on East Second Street, and in fact there was no reason he couldn't live like this for decades more. But it worried us that one night he'd get beaten up far worse than usual, or stumble into the street in front of a cab or a truck, or go into the river. Any one of a thousand disasters could befall a man who lived like Danny did in New York City. Were we just to wait until it happened? I said this. Agnes was still not convinced.

'There's a reason he does it,' she said.

She meant the nightmares, of course; the horror. I was reminded then of the culture of the house in which she'd grown up, the alcoholic father and the long-suffering mother who drank defensively. In such a house it was accepted that pain should be dulled with alcohol. The idea of anesthesia had strong valence in the unwritten code of the Magill household. Agnes was abstemious herself, but at some level she felt it was all right for Danny to drink as much as he did, and she condoned it. It was the effect the war had had on him she hated, not his response to it.

'But he's so confused right now,' she said.

'You'll apologize for him whatever he does.'

'He's all right when he comes here.'

She would make no demands of him. She would encourage him to drink if it deadened his pain. She hated that he was suffering and she didn't care how he dealt with it.

'I can't just stand by and let him go on like this,' I said. 'He does nothing useful.'

'Why should he do anything useful? Didn't he serve?'

She looked up at me as she licked a rolling paper. It was as though she had torn a curtain from a screen. Suddenly revealed before me was a picture I hadn't seen before. Danny went to Vietnam; I did not. Danny *served*. Five years later I would've handled such a thrust with tact, if I handled it at all. If it was a thrust. But I was young. I bridled. I responded with more heat than I needed to.

'So the war excuses him from all responsibility,' I snapped. 'Is that your point?'

'Keep your voice down.'

I calmed down. Agnes was pacing around

the kitchen, smoking, stopping at the window to stare at the street five stories below. Now she sat down opposite me and took my hands in hers.

'Are you sure about this, Charlie? Does Sam really think it's a good idea?'

'Will you trust me?'

Moment of truth. What was she to say? No, I won't, I won't trust you with the precarious balance of my brother's mind, I fear you'll be clumsy, you don't know enough, you'll blunder in and ruin everything. Did I see these thoughts flicker behind her eyes as she sat across the table from me, gripping my hands? Gazing at me with utter seriousness? But she didn't say anything. She should have, perhaps, though it would've done no good. It might have made things worse. She realized that as well.

I didn't see Danny again until the group met the next Thursday night. He seemed to have acquired no fresh injuries. The session ran about three hours, largely an ongoing discussion of Billy Sullivan seeing his buddy burned up beside him in the helicopter, and his insistence that it should have been him. I wanted to get at the thinking behind this. I also wanted Danny to see me give Billy some kind of resolution, a little peace, even, as a result of his willingness to open up.

'Why should it have been you, not your friend?'

'He was a good man,' said Billy.

'You're not?'

The other men sat listening, several of them leaning forward, staring at the floor, elbows on knees.

Billy sat back, gave a kind of hoot of laughter and turned to the other guys, grinning. He stretched his legs out in front of him and cocked his head to the side, gazing at me with the laughter dying now on his big sad bearded face. 'Ask me that in ten years, Doc.'

I glanced around the room. It was a warm night. Most of the other guys were grinning now, and even Danny had that look I'd seen once or twice, a softening of the features, an opening to something, anything, other than the vigilance of a man who expects at any moment to be ambushed, sniped at, booby-trapped, wasted.

Years later I had another patient, a woman of sixty, a judge, who told me that the world was no longer hospitable to human life. She grieved for her lost sense of security. She felt that her future was foreshortened, that she was living on borrowed time. This woman was sexually assaulted in her own chambers, and I remember her saying what Billy said.

She was a mature woman of high professional standing yet she couldn't think of herself as anything but worthless because she'd been raped. Because someone else had treated her as worthless. Toward the end of one of our early sessions she told me she felt she deserved it. She must have, she said. She'd been punished, and for good reason. I asked her if she recognized that this sort of thinking was pathological. She said it made no difference, it was how she felt. I then asked if she also felt that by talking about it she would eventually come to understand that she'd done nothing to deserve being raped. That's when she'd said what Billy had said: 'Ask me in ten years.'

I talked to Danny when the session ended. It was late, and I guessed he was ready for a drink. Part of the code to which he clung involved never showing up for the group other than sober. I knew what this cost him, and though we never spoke about it I imagined he held off out of respect for the others. He wanted to be a good witness, and this didn't go unremarked. Danny probably drank harder than any of these hard-drinking men but he held off on Thursdays until after the group. Not all of them were so responsible. I asked him if we could talk, just the two of us.

'Sure,' he said. 'We'll go to Smithy's.'

That was a bar, not what I had in mind. 'What about a cup of coffee instead?'

'I need a drink, Charlie.'

He lifted his eyebrows and touched his top lip with his tongue. His eyes were cold: arctic indifference, I sometimes saw it in him. He needed a drink. I acquiesced, thinking I had no choice. Smithy's was the place Agnes and I had gone to the first night she showed up at the hospital. It was an old-fashioned New York saloon, dark wood paneling, scuffed and splintered, a plank floor, a bored bartender, a few old men and some long-haired kids at a table by the jukebox. Framed photographs of old-time boxers on the wall. We sat at the far end of the counter on bar stools. It was smoky and hot. A ceiling fan turned listlessly overhead. Danny ordered bourbon with a chaser, I ordered a beer. I remember the words of the song on the jukebox. *We skipped the light fandango, turned cartwheels 'cross the floor,* something like that. I can never hear them now without thinking of that night.

'So what's up?'

'Here's the question,' I said.

A word I once heard used about myself in those days was *earnest.* I dislike the connotations — humorless, hectoring, persistent, dull. Perhaps Danny didn't see me like that.

176

I sat with my hands flat on the bar. Frowning and earnest, I asked, 'So what happened to you after your buddy got killed?'

Down went the bourbon, the shot glass pushed across the counter. Wordlessly, the bartender refilled it and picked what he needed from the heap of dollar bills I'd thrown down.

Danny spoke quietly, not looking at me. 'It didn't happen to me. I made it happen to them.'

'You want to tell me what you did?'

'You don't want to know.'

'Sure I do.'

I remember when I said this he looked straight at me, and this time his eyes weren't cold; instead they seemed to burn into my unseasoned, unknowing soul, and I was suddenly afraid. I was out of my depth. At the same time I was committed to what I was doing. I told myself it was good I was afraid. This was my work, and at last I was facing the real diseased part, the sickness in this man's mind. It didn't matter that we were in a shabby midtown saloon instead of the safe, formal setting of the basement room we'd just come from. He turned away, and his eyes in the mirror behind the bottles flickered to my mirrored eyes and held them for a second or two. There arose in him, or so I imagined, a desire to let the poison out.

'We didn't have to be there, Charlie.'

'Go on.'

He stared at the counter shaking his head. Did he mean Southeast Asia or the place where his buddy had died?

'Somebody fucked up. We shouldn't have been there.'

Then he lifted his head and turned back to me and pronounced the words slowly, swaying slightly on the bar stool, almost in a trance and as though chanting a mantra. He beat his fingers on the counter in time to the words. '*We didn't — have to — fucking — be there, man! We didn't have to be there!*'

Such weird and bitter fury in him as he said this, his fists clenched and eyes cast down. It was still so fresh that it might have happened yesterday. Now he was shaking his head. We sat in silence for some minutes.

'It all went to hell for me after that. I didn't care about any of it anymore. All I knew, the more of them I wasted the better I felt.'

'Killing made you feel good.'

'Less bad. Every time it got easier. And there was other stuff.'

He was drinking bourbon steadily and I had the impression of a spigot opened, the flow intermittent yet unstoppable. He was speaking rapidly but in tones so low it was difficult to understand him. The jukebox was loud, that didn't help, and the long-haired kids were getting rowdy. Danny didn't look at me, he just muttered at the counter, pushing the shot glass over, and I kept adding dollars to the soggy pile in front of us.

'Four months, Charlie, until they shipped me out of there. I was an animal, I just wanted to kill. And I messed with their bodies if I could get at them. That's not an animal, that's worse than an animal. Animals don't kill because they like it.'

'They kill to eat.'

He seemed all at once to awaken to his surroundings. *They kill to eat.* He looked around with a familiar expression, as though he was expecting at any moment to be attacked. He stared at the table by the jukebox. One of the kids shouted, 'What the fuck you looking at?' and I thought he was going to take them on. Abruptly he got off his stool and walked out of the bar onto the street. It happened so fast I was paralyzed for a few seconds. Then I went after him, looking up and down the sidewalk, but he was gone. He'd disappeared into the city. I went back into the bar.

'You want another?' said the bartender.

On the subway going home, sitting among the rolling beer cans and abandoned newspapers, staring at the ubiquitous spray-can graffiti and being eyed by the few wary passengers traveling that late in the evening, I tried to see the encounter in a positive light: I had got Danny talking. But I knew his abrupt departure wasn't good. Though I'd got him to open up some, I'd had no chance to give him any sort of help in handling the storm of feeling that came with the arousal of those memories. I doubt I could have comforted him; probably nobody could.

Or perhaps the group could. Sam Pike said this when I saw him the next day. Perhaps only the group could handle the fallout, when Danny allowed himself to remember. As it was he'd drink all night so as to drive off the demons, and I didn't want to think about that because I was responsible.

Agnes saw all this at once. 'What have you done?'

She was waiting up for me. Barely was I through the door than she was there, asking if I'd been with Danny. Yes, I told her wearily, I had.

'What happened?'

I was hot and irritated, and angry with myself. I'd been confronted with what I regarded as my own inadequacy. I couldn't explain my intimation that I'd done real harm, but Agnes saw it and she was horrified.

I told her how Danny had left the bar. I hadn't had the time or the guile to tailor my account. I told her the stark truth.

'I don't believe you could have been so *dumb*! You took him to a *bar*? To talk about *Vietnam*?'

I was aware of a cluster of reactions, none of them worthy. I didn't defend myself, nor did I attempt to minimize what had happened. I sat with my elbows on the table and my face in my hands.

'You'll just have to go find him.'

Unable to be still, she was pacing the kitchen with her arms folded tight across her chest. I put my hands on the table and lifted my face to where she stood gazing down at me, the dismay of a moment before now replaced by conviction. There was something to be done, after all.

'He could be anywhere.'

'Then I'll go,' she said.

She couldn't contemplate the prospect of doing nothing. One or the other of us had to go out into the night and of course it was me. Frayed and exhausted, bitterly angry with myself, I told her I wanted to change my shirt. Then I'd go over to the East Village and look for him.

'Bring him back here,' she said. 'I don't want him out there all night. Christ knows what he'll do. I'll tell you where to go, Charlie, go to Seventh and B and if he's not there ask Boone where he's drinking tonight.'

There followed a list of bars, above St. Mark's and below, in any of which Danny might be found. I changed my shirt and went out again. A hot summer night on the East Side brings people out of their apartments and into the streets, which were more crowded at midnight than they'd been at noon. The mood was festive on some blocks, sinister on others. At one in the morning the air was still hot, the sidewalks busy, traffic cruising and people screaming. Every time I was accosted, propositioned, threatened, I asked if Danny Magill had been around.

'Danny who, man? I don't know no Dan Magill, man. Yo! You know Dan Magill, right? No, man, don't nobody know no Dan Magill around here. What else you want?'

Some did know Danny, mostly bartenders, but nobody could be sure of having seen him that night. At four in the morning I was in a seedy joint on Rivington Street and had given up. I sat at the bar and drank a beer. There were after-hours places I could have checked out, but I saw no point. If he was in the neighborhood he'd be drunk by now, and there'd be little for me to do except try to make sure he didn't get hurt, and I had no idea how long he might tolerate that. Not long, was my guess. So I went home.

Agnes was still up. She was at the door at the first sound of my key in the lock. Her face, full of hope, at once collapsed.

'No good?'

'Nobody's seen him.'

'Okay,' she said. 'Bed.'

She had no more emotion left in her. She was empty, incapable of further anxiety until her body was replenished by rest. Within moments she was asleep. I lay in the warm darkness listening to the fan, watching the curtain stir as the whisper of a breeze went stealing by, and for a few seconds I entertained the notion that no harm had been done, that Danny had simply gone out drinking as usual, that he'd effectively locked down his nightmares and what had happened earlier was of no consequence. Agnes was just over-reacting. She was a little irrational when it came to her brother. All would be well. And thinking this, I fell asleep myself.

★ ★ ★

It was impossible to sustain that hope over the days that followed. Agnes announced the next morning that she was asking Maureen to take care of Cassie while she looked for

Danny. I didn't try to dissuade her. But I did attempt to convey something of the optimism I'd felt just before sleep the night before. She was having none of it.

'Don't bother,' she said. 'Don't even try to cheer me up.'

This was said with brisk disdain. She had expressed no anger in the morning, and I realized this wasn't because she'd decided I was blameless, that my impulse had been sound and I couldn't have known, nobody could, what the consequences would be. No, she expressed no anger only because there was no point. She'd come to that conclusion the night before while I was out trawling the bars. She had raged at me in her mind and wept tears of angry frustration at the sheer folly of the callow man she'd had the misfortune to marry, but she had come to terms with the new reality and knew that nothing would be gained by anger. She felt it, of course she did, and it fueled the manifest contempt in her voice. My instructions were to find out what Sam Pike had to offer.

I remember he swiveled his chair around from the window and gazed at me. 'Oh, Charlie. So what did you say? What triggered it?'

I recounted the conversation. There was a long silence. Finally he said it would've been better if I'd done it in the group. I was to let him know if Danny showed up at the apartment on the weekend.

He didn't show up at the apartment, and he didn't show up for the group the next Thursday night. This worried Sam, and it sure as hell worried me. Sam clearly hadn't anticipated that I'd attempt psychotherapy with Danny Magill in a bar. He might have shouted at me, told me what an idiot I was, and I wish he had. But he too saw no point. I think he realized that I understood the scale of my blunder. He'd asked me almost at once how Agnes had reacted and he nodded when I told him, as if that's what he'd expected. But all he said by way of reproach was to repeat that he wished I'd done it in the group. By this point of course I wished the same thing; in fact there was nothing I wished for more ardently. My own stupidity astounded me. What had I been *thinking?* I'd been thinking, *My god, Danny will talk to me, and if he wants to talk in a bar, then so be it.* But I wouldn't have tried this with any of the other men. It was because he was Agnes's brother.

When he didn't appear on Thursday night, someone said, 'Where's Danny?' and I was alert for any reply that might shed light. I wanted to hear one of them, Billy Sullivan, I hoped, say he'd seen him the day before, they'd gone out to the track, or taken in a movie. But there was nothing. Sam Pike showed up, this his first appearance in a fortnight, and I didn't have to ask him why. Even so, I was unable to concentrate on the discussion. Sam opened the meeting by apologizing for missing the last two sessions, then summarized the group's concerns the last time he'd been with us. I told him about Billy's account of losing his copilot, and his belief that he should have died instead.

'I understand that,' said Sam. 'So what happened then?'

Billy started to talk, and his words reminded me of what Danny had said in the bar. I'd sensed there was more he wanted to tell me, and that it was those memories that had driven him out into the night. I tried to imagine how the evening might have gone had I handled it differently. When he'd told me we were going to a bar, if I had insisted we just wait until the room was empty and talk there, and if I had then suggested that I ask him some questions next week with the group present —

But now there was this hideous uncertainty surrounding him, and a mounting anxiety. We knew he'd been back to Second Street on at least a couple of occasions because he'd been seen in the building, though Agnes never found him home. And he had no telephone. Her anger remained steady, though still unspoken. I had the feeling that when this was all over, when Danny had finished driving everybody crazy and we could breathe again, then I'd hear exactly how she felt.

Sam was talking about loss of compassion in the wake of a friend's death, and from loss of compassion he moved on to loss of humanity. I put Danny out of my mind and concentrated on what was being said.

★　★　★

The call came on the Sunday. It had always been Danny's bad day. His worst hangovers occurred on Sundays. The city was quiet then, places were closed and a man alone was forced in on himself in ways he wasn't any other day of the week. I might have known it would be a Sunday. I took the call early that morning. Agnes was still asleep. It was Danny's neighbor on Second Street. She said I should come at once.

When I got home some hours later I made Agnes sit down at the table and then told her what had happened. I have never since that day seen such anguish on a woman's face. In my work I deal with the effects of trauma, but

I am never present when the damage actually happens. That morning I saw a woman to whom the worst thing she could imagine apart from her child dying had just occurred. She simply stared at me with her hands clenched tight on the table, shaking her head slightly, the tears streaming unchecked down her face. She reached for me and I held her as she wept. I'd found him in his room. He'd blown his brains out. I'd had to kick the door in.

12

Sometimes a failed relationship will confirm in a man a suspicion of his incapacity to sustain intimacy. I fell into this trap. In fact for some time after the end of my marriage I held fast to this belief, and saw no real reason to challenge it: I was unable to save anything. Even had I wanted to keep my marriage alive I doubt I could have succeeded. The fact was, since I could no longer face Agnes after what happened, I thought it best to end the marriage as quickly as possible. She despised me for this and I suppose I despised myself, which is of course a feature of depression. I remember telling her that she'd be better off without me, better able to get on with her life. The inadequacy of this as justification for leaving her was made very clear to me. I tried to explain how corrosive it would be, her conviction of my responsibility for Danny's death.

'Then change my conviction,' she said.

We were all in shock, me most of all. I'd been the first one into the apartment. I'd seen what that gunshot had done to his head, and I couldn't forget it. At least I had the distraction of the funeral arrangements and of contacting the men in the group. None of them blamed me. None of them was surprised. They were upset, they were saddened and angered, but not surprised. At the time we were only just starting to realize what this war would cost in terms of suicides. Years later, by chance, I ran into Billy Sullivan as I was coming out of a movie theater on Sixth Avenue. Life had not been kind to Billy. He walked with a stick and wheezed badly. He was maybe a hundred pounds overweight. His skin was red and flaking, his long hair thin and sparse. He had trouble on the sidewalk, this bulky, wheezing man. He cursed pedestrians who brushed against him in their haste. We went for a beer and talked about Danny, as well as two other men who'd turned their guns on themselves. Billy had been down to Washington to see the Vietnam War Memorial.

'You know how many names they got on that thing?'

I came up with a rough approximation.

'More than that have killed themselves.'

I went to see my mother and she at once connected Danny's suicide to our own relationship, hers and mine.

'Ah, Charlie,' she said. 'Always trying to help people who don't want it.'

We were in her apartment. It was about six in the evening, and she'd been drinking. I remembered her spectacles, black-rimmed and thick-lensed, hanging on her bosom from a piece of string. Her skin was gray, but her eyes were as sharp and bitter as her mind; she had yet to suffer the series of strokes that eventually destroyed the force indomitable.

'That's why you're in this line of work, isn't it, Charlie? You like getting into other people's private business. You like to intrude.'

Where did this come from? I wasn't ready for it. I'd thought I'd find sympathy here, for I sure as hell couldn't find it anywhere else. 'But *you* needed me,' I said.

'I never needed you. You just interfered. You were always interfering with me, same as with that poor boy, and now see what you've done.'

'I think I have to leave Agnes.'

'You sure do. Smartest thing you've said yet.'

I never understood why she hated Agnes, since she'd never showed any possessiveness toward me.

A few minutes later, after she'd had another drink, she told me she wasn't surprised. 'You're just like your father,' she said. 'Just walk away, why don't you? You got another woman already?'

I couldn't take any more of it and told her I didn't realize I'd injured her so badly. She was sitting forward in her chair, her elbow on her knee and her forehead pressed into her fingers, which held a lit cigarette, the other hand clawed around her glass. At these words her head came up and she stared at me. She seemed shocked. Then, inexplicably, tears were coursing down her cheeks. 'You didn't injure me, Charlie,' she said hoarsely, 'it was me. I injured you.'

'No — '

But she was already making for the door, head down, glasses dangling, one arm flapping at me to leave her alone. I followed her to her bedroom, where the familiar drama played out, me at the door asking to be let in, her inside weeping. But this time she wouldn't unlock the door. I sat in the living room with the lights off but she didn't come out of her room. It was after ten when I left.

I remember nothing of the funeral, although I have a vivid recollection of what was the first of many visits I've paid over the years to the city morgue, the Office of the Chief Medical Examiner, this one to identify Danny's remains, which came up from the basement on a metal gurney. They'd cleaned him up but again I had to look at the mess he'd made of his head. It did more than haunt me, it became yoked in my psyche to the guilt I felt. And the memory did not fade or change; it returned with all the immediacy and specificity of the experience itself, usually in my dreams. It is hell to remember like this, to possess a memory that will not decay. Back at the apartment Agnes was sunk deep in grief, and we moved around each other in almost total silence. Maureen cooked food that nobody wanted to eat and brewed pots of coffee nobody wanted to drink. I had already decided that I would move out at the beginning of September.

Agnes didn't speak to me for two years after Danny's death. When I visited Fulton Street she was never there, still too angry to be in the same room with me. Cassie was happy to see me regardless. Often we went swimming. There was a pool at NYU to which I had access. It was one of the very few pleasures I can remember from this period, splashing around with my daughter as I taught her how to swim. She was a leggy, slender child even then, and she was physically graceful. She loved being in the water and loved showing off. I remember one weekend when she was staying at my apartment, and our plan was to go to the pool early on Saturday morning and swim before breakfast. I think she was four. She was very excited, and we went to bed early. But during the night I was awoken. She was standing beside my bed, shaking me.

'Daddy, wake up! It's time!'

'It's the middle of the night, Cass.'

I struggled up and turned on the lamp on the night table. She had tried to put on her swimsuit, a little thing in shocking pink with shoulder straps, but she hadn't succeeded. It was somehow both upside down and backward and hopelessly twisted, her head sticking out through an armhole and her arms where her legs should be. There she stood in her little pink straitjacket, clapping her hands and telling me to get up or we'd be late.

'Come here, honey, what *have* you done?'

'We have to hurry, Daddy!'

Being with her at times made me feel wretched when I thought of what I had lost; what it was to have a family, what it was to be alone. Sometimes she burst into tears when I took her back to Fulton Street and told her I had to leave her now, and it broke my heart too. But Maureen was good. She would sweep the child up and comfort her, and while she was distracted I slipped away. At other times she was asleep when I came to the apartment, and I'd sit in the kitchen with Maureen. I was curious that she didn't hold me responsible for her brother's death, as Agnes did. Her reply surprised me. She said it was obvious Danny would die young.

'Agnes never told me that,' I said.

'Well, she wouldn't, would she?'

'What do you mean?'

'She worshipped him. She couldn't contemplate it.'

Maureen was heavier and softer than Agnes, a statuesque woman with thick coppery hair who for some weeks had dated Billy Sullivan. The men in the group gave Billy plenty of grief for claiming that because of Maureen Magill he was 'mellow.' She let him go when he started to get weird on her, as she put it, but she let him down lightly and they stayed friendly. I admired the tact with which she did it. So when she told me she'd always known Danny would die young, I paid close attention.

'He had demons,' she said, 'even when he was a little kid. What a moody kid! It would come on him so suddenly, and we just had to get out of the way. He was the same as Daddy like that.'

We were drinking coffee and waiting for Cassie to wake up from her nap. Maureen dressed like a hippie, all flowing skirts and scarves and beads. She was as impressive a personality as her sister but she inclined to the role of earth mother, which Agnes emphatically did not. Like Agnes she rolled her own cigarettes, though with weed mixed in.

'Go on,' I said.

'Oh, he'd do all this crazy stuff.'

'Like what?'

'Like one time he jumped into an old quarry. Nobody knew how deep the water was, but he didn't care. I'll never forget it. It was a long way down and we watched him, a bunch of us kids, and we didn't know and he didn't know if the water was two feet deep or what. Agnes was a mess.'

I could picture it, the young Danny sauntering to the edge of the quarry, bare-chested, barefoot, freckles on his shoulders, gazing down at the still, brown water, drowsy with insects and sparkling where sunlight came dappling through the foliage above. Small boys gathered around their leader, proud but secretly horrified; it was for the boys that he was doing it. Then shouting 'Geronimo' — jumping — and coming up spluttering in the sunshine, his arms up over his head, and the children at the top of the cliff dancing around and yelling, all but one of them ecstatic at his bold feat, and the one not yelling was Agnes, for whom it was too much, he could have been *killed* —

And all at once I saw her crying for him in our bed at night, and me not there to comfort her. Me not there.

★ ★ ★

Another time I asked Maureen if Danny was really the hero who stood up for his mother and sisters when their father came home drunk and wanted to hit someone. She shook her head.

'It was you?' I said.

'It was Agnes.'

He would come home and want to hit his son, and it was Agnes who prevented him, Agnes who took the slaps herself. But she'd turned the story upside down. She'd told it as she'd wanted it to happen, that Danny defended *her*, and I think by then she believed it.

'It wasn't your fault he killed himself,' Maureen said, blowing smoke at the ceiling.

'Agnes thinks it was.'

'She thinks that now.'

At first I thought my clinical career was over. I'd made up my mind to quit the unit. And in the bleak, selfish spirit with which I'd abandoned my marriage I considered this a good thing. I spoke to Sam Pike about it. He confirmed what Maureen had said, that

Danny was always a suicide risk.

He became dogmatic, prodding the table with his finger. 'It was *not* your fault. You did *not* drive him to it. It had very little to do with that botched intervention of yours. Anything might have triggered it. Try not to play the martyr here, Charlie.'

We were having lunch in the oyster bar in Grand Central. Sam had a train to catch. He was speaking at an antiwar rally someplace upstate. He was constantly on the move in those years.

'No reason it shouldn't make you a better therapist.'

'*Better?*'

'If you can learn from it. You shouldn't have left Agnes but I guess that's not my business.'

'You're right,' I said. 'It's not.'

He busied himself with his lobster, cracking a claw and clumsily extracting the meat. Sam loved to eat but he wasn't elegant about it. He encouraged me not to give up, and in the further course of the conversation — it was, in retrospect, one of the more important conversations of my life — he not only succeeded in convincing me to stay on at the unit, but fired my imagination with his vision of an emerging discipline. He meant the treatment of trauma. He was already using the term *posttraumatic syndrome*.

'Charlie, I want you with me. What's the time? I must go.'

'You want me?' I said, rising from the table.

'You're young,' he said. 'I'm not.'

He threw down some bills and went shouldering out, flinging an arm up in farewell. I sat back down at the table. It was now clear that I could, after all, be useful — that I too could serve. Otherwise I did not know what the point of me was. And after Danny's death, to have a point was a matter of some considerable importance.

But Sam was right, I now realize; I shouldn't have left Agnes. In my blindness and selfishness I had looked to my own pain and not to hers. I was wretched after I moved out; the memory of those days still makes me ashamed. There was all the nuisance of physical upheaval — getting my books out of Fulton Street was a nightmare, in the heat — but worse, of course, far worse was the wrench of separation. Agnes was at times so very vulnerable, so pathetic and childlike in her desperation, that it took an inhuman level of detachment for me to go through with it. But I did it. Somehow I managed to raise the cold determination to see it through, and I functioned like a machine, impervious to her misery. Within a month I was able to glimpse the extent of my cruelty but by then it was too late, or so I thought. With a kind of grim relish I settled to my suffering, and my awareness of Agnes's suffering only served to twist the knife already deep in my guts.

It later occurred to me that by failing Agnes I had again failed my mother. I'd behaved exactly as Fred had. But did I want to fail my mother? Did I have to? Because I hated her? We see nobody clearly. We see only the ghosts of absent others, and mistake for reality the fictions we construct from blueprints drawn up in early childhood. This is the problem.

★ ★ ★

Agnes asked me over for dinner again. I'd been to see Joe Stein in the afternoon. They still didn't know if he would walk again. When I asked how he felt he said he felt sore, how the hell did I think he felt? But I detected a change in him. I didn't see, as I have in others who have failed in a suicide attempt, the steely conviction that next time will be different, next time they'll do it right. There was a new attitude in Joe Stein, I thought, as though he had paid, or at least was paying, and perhaps this was all — having taken a life — that he'd wanted to do. As though he had offered his own life in good faith, and the offer had been declined. It wasn't the time to speak of such things, but all the same I had the sense that we'd both just glimpsed the possibility of an end to our suffering, for I was then raising the question with Agnes of whether we might try again, she and I. Before I left I asked Stein how his wife was.

'Guardedly pessimistic,' he said.

Guardedly pessimistic — was that me? No. I allowed myself to soar higher than that. I had hope. I thought I could undo the error that had robbed me of seven years with Agnes. I thought I could go home, and in fact I saw no reason why I shouldn't. I had been much buoyed by what had happened at Sam's memorial, and while I was aware of the unreliability of one's peers' approbation, the salutary effect on my parched ego of being reminded of my professional status was nonetheless profound. I stood at the window in my apartment and told myself that my life was about to change. I put on the glorious Schubert E-flat Piano Trio, sank into an armchair and closed my eyes. That night I slept well and awoke with the mood intact.

I heard nothing from Nora. I felt sorry about how it had worked out, sorry that she'd failed to find what she was after. She would never find it, of course, not without psychotherapy, for what she wanted was a man to whom she could submit while he treated her, and whom she could at the same time punish for what he, or rather that absent other of whom he was the ghost, had done to her in the past.

13

August, and the weather continued hot and humid, unrelenting days of gas fumes, fraying tempers, sirens, fire trucks and garbage in the streets. Human wreckage everywhere you looked. In City Hall Park, just yards from the mayor's office, I watched a kid on a bench shoot up with heroin and then doze off. I was still seeing Cassie on the weekends. I'd pick her up at Fulton Street in the morning and over an early lunch we'd discuss what she wanted to do. I didn't tell her of my recent efforts to displace Leon and resume being her daddy full-time, and I was certain Agnes wouldn't speak to her about it either. But I forgot what a very perceptive child she was.

'Are you coming to live with us again?'

We were having lunch in her favorite place, a diner on Tenth Avenue. There was a long counter with fixed stools, and tables and banquettes by the window. From the grill came the sizzle of frying bacon. Food orders were being shouted back and forth, all was briskness and gruff conviviality. She'd ordered a burger and fries. I was having a coffee.

'I'm not, honey.'

She gazed at me through half-closed eyes, an expression meant to communicate shrewd penetration. 'Mommy told Leon you weren't moving back in so he should just stop worrying.'

I said I couldn't move back in if Leon was living there. Two daddies in the same apartment? My tone was one of elaborate reasonableness.

Cass frowned. 'I wish you would.'

I'd always made it a point never to talk to Cassie about Leon. I'd told Agnes years before that if we used our daughter to spy on each other, it would be hard on her for all kinds of reasons.

'But you want to, don't you?' she said.

'There's no point talking about what can't happen.'

'Why can't it happen?'

It was torture, having to pretend like this. I refused to cut off the conversation by telling her a lie, by saying that no, I didn't want to move back in. At the same time I couldn't tell her that I *did*, though this, naturally, was what she needed to know. She needed to know where I stood. Cass was very like her mother in some respects, she had Agnes's directness and obstinacy.

She shrugged. 'I'll find out anyway,' she said.

Another time we were in a cab going north on the FDR and I was staring out the window at the river. I was a thousand miles away.

'Are you sad today, Daddy?'

'Sorry, Cass, I'm preoccupied.'

'You look sad. Is it because of Leon?'

'No.'

'Mommy is.'

This was the sort of statement we had agreed we would not follow up on. It was none of my business if Agnes was sad about Leon. I couldn't care less how she felt about her fireman.

'He's sick, that's why Mommy's sad.'

'Honey, I never talk to you about Leon. You should know that by now.'

Then I saw there was something else going on. She was frightened. I couldn't have the conversation with her, but I could attend to her feelings. There in the back of the cab I opened my arms, and gratefully she let herself be folded into a hug. I stroked her hair. Whatever was going on at home was disturbing her and so I comforted her, telling her she was a strong girl and that she would be able to handle it, whatever happened. When we reached the park she'd recovered, and we set off to find a hot dog stand. She was a skinny kid but she ate like a horse.

A few days later I returned to Fulton

Street. Cassie was staying over at Maureen's and Leon was out somewhere, so it was just Agnes and me. Leon so often seemed to be out, and this I took to be a sign of the breakdown of the marriage, though Agnes would never talk about it.

'Charlie, I've been thinking,' she said.

We were seated at the kitchen table. There was a salmon in the oven. She was looking very attractive, I thought, in her casual, lanky fashion. I said so. She asked if I wanted music and I told her I didn't care, and she said that with the others out she was happy to have silence.

I'd been thinking too. I'd allowed myself to indulge a domesticity fantasy. The idea of membership in a family again, this aroused me strongly, and while with one part of my brain I watched my emotions with cautious detachment, at the same time I periodically surrendered to giddy speculation. So I was at times a fevered youth, and at other times the watchful parent of that youth.

'I've been thinking,' she said, 'about what you said about wanting to come back. Were you serious?'

'I was. I am.'

She gazed at me, then laid her head against the back of the chair and pushed her hands through her hair and sighed. Agnes had lovely slim hands with long, tapering fingers. I had always loved her hands.

'You said you didn't know me anymore.'

'What I meant was I've missed so much that's happened to you.'

'People don't change, Charlie.'

'Not without help we don't.'

She frowned. She was scrutinizing me.

'I think you do know me. But I don't know you anymore, that's the point. When Danny died, when you left me, I didn't understand why you were doing it. I didn't recognize what made you do it. I thought you'd go away for a few days, even a week or two, and then you'd come back. And I was bewildered, this on top of everything else in my life just then, and it turned to anger. And I was angry with you for a long time.'

'I know.'

'But you didn't do anything about it.'

'I know.'

'But *why?*'

She was sitting forward now, her hands laid flat on the table. She stared at me and I saw that she was genuinely unable to understand why I'd hurt her so badly. I saw too that my response to this mattered very much.

'Many reasons. Shame. Despair. Sense of spiritual fragmentation. Alienation. I didn't start to come out of it till the night of Mom's funeral.'

'So you've said.'

'And when I saw that instead of sparing you I'd betrayed you by not being there when you needed me, I felt even worse. I felt I wasn't fit to be with you.'

'Or anybody else, apparently. Until this Nora.'

I didn't challenge this.

'And you haven't been in therapy, you of all people!'

'No.'

'And now you come back as though nothing happened.'

'I don't pretend that nothing happened.'

'But what if you get depressed again? And decide you're not fit to live with? Will you walk out on us like you did before?'

'No.'

A silence here. She didn't ask how I could be sure of it, though the question hung in the air anyway.

'I know what I want now,' I said.

She frowned. 'I'm too old for experiments, Charlie.'

I said nothing to this. I waited.

'I need to know you're with me for good before I let you back in.'

The fevered youth in my head had crawled

into some dark place and was not to be heard from. I reviewed whatever occurred to me to say and none of it seemed adequate. 'I don't know what I can tell you other than this,' I said, 'that I'll never hurt you again. I don't know how to make you believe that.'

'You believe it?'

'I do.'

She sipped her wine and gazed at me. There was a *ping!* from the oven but she ignored it. All at once I saw that she wanted to believe me, that there lived in her, if not a fevered youth, then a woman who could still love poor Charlie Weir but was taking counsel from a parent urging caution, reminding her of what had happened the last time she'd allowed herself to love him.

'I need you, and I want to deserve your love. Nothing's more important to me than that.'

'Charlie.'

I looked for the change in her body, in her fingers, that would tell me I had reached her, touched her, but she was still. Then she sank back in the chair again and covered her mouth with her hand. Her eyes still gazed steadily at me and the light caught a dampness in them. She wanted to believe, but she resisted. She was covering her mouth to stop herself from saying something rash.

Another *ping!* from the oven.

'We should eat,' she said, but still she didn't move. 'You're a very lonely man.'

'I didn't know how lonely until now.'

'That's what I'm afraid of. There's still a bit missing, Charlie.'

This again. 'What do you mean, a bit missing?' I said. 'What is it, heart, soul? Or *you! You're* what's missing!'

She shrugged. But I was incomplete, she was right, and it was because I was alone, and desperate to escape my aloneness. This didn't help my cause. I could hardly tell her that I wanted her back so as not to be alone anymore, but she knew that that's what it was. It wasn't about her needs then but mine, my need to complete myself. Or escape from myself.

'You think that's why I'm here?' I said.

Her eyes weren't damp anymore.

'Because you're lonely? Yes, I do.'

Another silence. Another *ping!*

'We should eat.'

This time she got up and as she passed my chair she laid her fingers on my shoulder and I seized them. The next thing, she was in the chair with me, in my arms and clutching me, and I could feel the anger in her, confused anger, and desire. She kissed me as I ran my hands across her back and down her hips, then suddenly she pushed away from me and stood up, panting slightly, and I couldn't tell if she was about to laugh or cry.

'I'm not ruining that fish for you,' she said.

While we ate we talked about Cassie, about Agnes's work and about Danny, how her grief was at times as fresh as it had been the day he died. She told me she no longer believed it was my fault he killed himself. She now accepted that it would've happened anyway. She had never said this to me before, and I was astonished that she did now. But my response was dampened by the knowledge that this was not what really mattered to her. What mattered was that I'd left her.

'So you could have stayed,' she said. 'It would have been all right in the end.'

'I couldn't see it then.'

'No, you couldn't.'

Leon was due home about nine, so I left a little before then. At the door she kissed me and told me to look after myself.

'We'll keep talking,' I said.

'Oh, I'm sure we will,' she said, closing the door on me.

I walked up Fulton Street to the subway. My mood was somber, the exhilaration I'd felt earlier now dissipated. But I wasn't defeated yet. And at least I'd learned that she wanted to be convinced that I could love her properly and for good.

14

The next day Nora called me at my office. I knew our break wouldn't be entirely clean, that she would require at least one conversation to justify to herself what she'd done. I didn't intend to argue with her. I would urge her to seek help elsewhere, and give her the name of a colleague if she wanted it. I might suggest that the content of the nightmares indicated repressed trauma stemming from incidents in her childhood. On the phone she told me she'd left a few things behind, including her keys to the apartment. So she couldn't get in. Could she stop by this evening and pick them up?

'Of course,' I said.

It was an uncomfortably warm day, damp and sultry. The city was tense and I felt a simmering antagonism whenever I was out on the street. I had Elly in the afternoon, and we had reached a complicated stage. After the session when she'd proposed that we have sex I'd spent some time attempting to persuade her that I was there not to replicate her relationship with her father but to enable her to come to terms with it, or rather to *recover* from it. I'd been working hard to convince her that here in my office she would come to no harm. I was reminded of that comment of Billy Sullivan's, years back, when he'd said, 'No safe place, man.'

Elly was one of those for whom there was no safe place. Here was a woman whose bedroom when she was growing up wasn't the haven within the home that every child needs. Night after night she had lain awake and waited for the door to crack open, for light from the upstairs landing to slide into the room, and with it the figure of a man in silhouette: her father. She told me later that when he came in she went out, by which she meant she left her body. She became expert at dissociating from the experience and watching as though from a high place, the corner of the ceiling, she said, what happened to the girl on the bed.

Later, as a teenager, when her father went instead to her sister's room, she became anorexic, and eventually she was hospitalized. This was all in the case notes. So alarmed did the medical staff become by her refusal to eat that they tried feeding her through a tube. And when she tore out the tube, they strapped her into a chair and forced it down her throat.

This truly shocked me, that her doctors

could be so criminally stupid as to hold her down against her will and push a tube into her mouth. This was what her father had done to her, pushed his tube into her mouth; it had caused the anorexia in the first place. So I knew it would be slow. But she trusted me now, and it was time for her to start talking about what had happened. It was time for her to remember.

I met fierce resistance. 'No, Dr. Weir, I don't want to remember, don't make me!' I allowed long silences. There were tears. Toward the end of each session I pulled back, leading her to safe ground, her life in the present, the relationship she'd formed with another prosecutor in the D.A.'s office, an older woman. This was familiar territory, and she was able to talk about the woman without becoming upset. She even laughed a little when she described their last date. She left my office with some confidence; she was looking forward, she said, to our next session. I saw her out myself. I could no longer afford a full-time receptionist.

But I was exhausted. It becomes no easier, dealing with damage of this magnitude. And it was an effort to suppress my anger at what had been done to Elly. Moral outrage doesn't help much. You must be sensitive every second to the nuanced message the patient is sending. Is she ready to take the next step? Is this the moment to press her, to try to break through the denial and expose the horror of what has been repressed? Or is it time to pull back, review progress, consolidate? This is my work. I do it well. But it's exhausting.

The subway was crowded, and it was a drained and listless Charlie Weir who emerged at Twenty-third Street. I didn't relish seeing Nora, or for that matter anyone at all. I had a nice piece of pork tenderloin. I would boil a little rice, maybe some green beans, and have a simple dinner by myself. I had a new recording of sonatas that Mozart wrote in Munich when he was nineteen, and I knew they would purge the dross of the day. But instead of Wolfgang Amadeus I could look forward only to Nora Chiara. I took a shower, changed my clothes, poured myself a small scotch and settled down with the paper until she arrived.

I buzzed her up and she stood in the doorway looking smaller than when I'd last seen her, that ghastly evening at Sulfur when Walt told me I wasn't alive.

'Come in.'

'You're drinking, Charlie. What's happened?'

She was nervous. She had often urged me to drink more. She'd have liked a man who went with her glass for glass. I poured her some wine. She took off her coat and hung it on the back of a chair. She made no move to collect her belongings and instead perched on a stool at the kitchen counter.

'How's Audrey?' I said.

'Oh, they're very generous, but I feel like such a refugee. I can't impose on them much longer.'

I'd begun to see Nora's chronic homelessness as a symptom of her pathology. There was a void in the woman and she tried to fill it by having others take her in and care for her. She lit a cigarette. I'd finally got the smell of her last cigarettes out of the apartment, and she detected my displeasure. I felt too tired to act gallant about her tobacco habit.

'I'm sorry. Do you want me to go out on the fire escape?'

There had been times in the last month or so when I'd asked her to smoke out there. Then one night she'd said it wasn't safe. The bolts in the railing were corroded with rust. She told me I should speak to the super about it, or if not the super then I should report it to the city. I'd done nothing of the sort, and that had been the pretext for another fight.

'No, it's all right,' I said. 'Smoke away. So

what are your plans?'

'I thought we might talk about that, Charlie. My plans.'

'Go on,' I said.

'Don't be cold. This is very hard for me. I know I've been a bitch, but you haven't exactly been a saint.'

'I never claimed to be a saint.'

'Nor did I.'

I'd already guessed what was coming and I didn't like it one bit. This was all happening way too fast. She hadn't been in the apartment ten minutes.

'Could I have some more wine?'

I poured her a little more. I wanted her sober for this.

'We can't just — '

'We can't just what?'

'Charlie! Help me here!'

She sat perched on the stool looking helpless and fragile and vulnerable and, yes, beautiful. There was always that, and with it my damn body responding. My body would betray me in a second, and it took all my will to stay on my own side of the kitchen counter and watch her with the appearance of if not indifference then sympathy. Distanced sympathy.

'Can't we just try again?'

The irony was not lost on me: of human

bondage, this was the motif, the cruel awareness that the very form of supplication I'd used with Agnes was now being employed on me. 'It wouldn't be any different if we did,' I said. 'You really have to deal with your problems.' I said this with reasonableness and concern. And in a tone of regret.

'But I will. I've been thinking about it all week. The offer you made me, the short course of therapy? I'll do it. If only to mend things between us.'

'It's too late.' Oh, this cost me. This was harsh. To be so harsh when all I wanted was to unbutton her blouse.

'No, it's not!' She stood up, her face so naked in its appeal, so desperately weak and frightened. 'Please don't say it's too late!'

She came around the end of the counter and lay her head against my chest and wept. I put my arms around her, but loosely. I wanted her, but I couldn't allow it, had I not made my choice? Was I not fighting for my life here? I took her by the shoulders and pushed her away. She stood there for a moment, so small and perfect, with her hair falling over her downturned face, and then gave a kind of damp sigh and turned and walked to the far end of the room and stood with her back to me. I came around the counter and hitched myself onto a stool and watched her, waiting.

She spoke without turning. 'I know you don't mean it.'

'I'm afraid I do.'

I thought, ludicrously, of a painting of St. Stephen the Martyr, that androgynous boy with the arrows in his body. Another dart had just pierced Nora's flesh. She seemed the martyr now, myself the instrument of her martyrdom. But had I not made my choice?

She walked across the room toward me. She came close and took my hands where they lay unmoving on my thighs. 'You really don't care anymore?'

Her closeness nearly undid me. Inside this impassive man there raged a bloody civil war. I had to lie to her. Had I not made my choice? 'It's not the point if I care or not.'

'But do you?'

'It's not about what I want.'

Then it all changed.

'It's *not about* what *you want!*'

Spoken, or spat, rather, with contempt. All at once I felt my exhaustion. I didn't have the wherewithal to go on with this and I told her so. But she was already in the spare room getting her things. When she emerged she was still very upset, and I didn't want her to leave like this; she should calm down before she went out on the street. But she wouldn't answer me, she wouldn't even look at me, and she sure as hell wouldn't let me ride down in the elevator with her. Then she was gone. I didn't feel right about what had happened. I went into the spare room. She had taken her things and also her keys to the apartment. I sat on the bed and cursed.

In the days that followed I tried to calculate what all this meant. I heard nothing more from her, nor from Agnes. I wanted to tell Agnes what had happened, but I was unwilling to engage her support as I negotiated what I thought of as the death throes of my relationship with Nora. That is, if she'd even offer her support, and if indeed these were the death throes. I couldn't assume that Nora would go quietly, and I knew I'd have to expect at least one more attempt to change my mind. By unintentionally arousing her contempt I might well have hammered the last or next-to-last nail in the coffin, though with Nora you could be sure of nothing. I strongly suspected I would again be forced to be cruel.

★ ★ ★

Then the ax fell. Of human bondage: having rejected Nora with what I thought was finality, on Friday I called Agnes. Her tone

220

was cool and measured and she didn't spare my feelings. She said I was driven by loneliness and isolation, not by love, and she had no confidence that I wouldn't hurt her again. She didn't believe I'd changed in any fundamental way.

'I'm not prepared to take the risk, Charlie.'

'But there's Cassie — '

'You can still see Cassie.'

I protested, of course I did. I said she had to give me a chance. I put up strong arguments and told her she was wrong, that I *had* changed, and knew what I wanted now, which was to be with my family. I would be loving, supportive, faithful —

'Faithful isn't your strong suit, Charlie.'

This was unfair; it was with *her* that I'd been unfaithful! I told her I was finished with Nora. I said I couldn't live without her.

'You lived without me for seven years.'

'And it was hell!'

'I don't think so. I knew you'd do this. Please don't. It only makes it harder for me.'

She didn't flinch. There was no sympathy for my distress, no wavering, no opening to any possibility of compromise or delay. She wouldn't meet me to discuss it further. She wouldn't sleep on it, having slept on it already. This went on for several minutes, then all at once I gave up. There was no point. She had made her decision. She knew her own mind. I felt sick. I felt fatalistic. I felt *nihilistic*. I sat at my desk with my head in my hands. I went into the washroom and stared at myself in the mirror. I had planned to take her to *Faust*, which was being performed at Lincoln Center on Saturday night, and now I had to go alone. For the first time in a long while I couldn't lose myself in that most darkly exhilarating of operas. I was unable to attend either to what was happening onstage or to the restless movement of my own thoughts. I was caught instead in some middle ground of distracted despair from which violent impulses erupted. I emerged onto the plaza and walked south on Broadway among the Saturday night crowds.

It was loud on the street that Saturday night, almost deafening, all the roaring and wailing and screaming. From Columbus Circle I continued south on Eighth Avenue. There were theatergoers emerging from shows that had just let out, and dealers in doorways and scuzzy-looking characters hanging around sex arcades. There were garbage cans kicked over, the trash spilling out across the sidewalk. The closer I got to Forty-second Street the seedier the neighborhood became, but I didn't give a damn anymore.

I found what I was looking for somewhere

west of Times Square, where in an empty lot at the end of a deserted street a Cadillac was sitting on blocks. The doors were off, the wheels and engine gone, but the backseat was intact and a woman sat there smoking in the shadows. I clambered through a hole in the fence, conscious only of a quickening hunger for cathartic sex.

15

It is from this night that I date my decline. I had begun to entertain domesticity scenarios in which Cassie once again had her real father, and Agnes and I grew old together. I was astonished at how hard it hit me, the destruction of this fantasy. It was particularly bad at night. After a period of quiescence the old disorder was awakened, and I felt it stirring in the darkness like a beast in its den. In the years I'd been treating trauma I'd learned this, that when ordinary anxiety becomes sufficiently acute it will rouse the dormant horror no matter how deeply repressed it is. I began dreaming about Danny again, and though I suppose I should have consulted someone, I was resistant to the idea. There was a perverse hubris attached to this: none of my colleagues enjoyed such intimate contact with the disorder. And now I felt it moving again.

Monday was another very humid day and I had an appointment in the afternoon with Joe Stein. I found him in wry humor. I must have looked wretched.

'You jump out a window too?'

I sat down at his bedside. He was strapped into a molded plastic body jacket to keep his trunk immobilized. Stein was extraordinary. Any other man in his situation would be struggling with forms of humiliation connected to basic bodily functions, and also anxious about his sexual future. You expect a man to be depressed, if he's sustained a spinal-cord injury like Stein's; but he was upbeat. I could only conclude that I'd been right about him, that he'd absolved himself of the death of the pedestrian. He'd offered himself, he could do no more than that, and now he'd take life on any terms, even as a paraplegic. I asked him if his wife was still guardedly pessimistic.

'Oh sure, I'd be alarmed if she were anything but.'

'I saw her in the corridor.'

'She say anything?'

'It wasn't what she said.'

This gave him pleasure.

I stood outside the hospital and contemplated walking over to Fulton Street, and then I remembered: she wanted nothing more to do with me. It was all about my needs and not about hers. Despite my protestations to the contrary I hadn't changed. *I'm too old for experiments, Charlie.*

My patients were my distraction, my solace, my sanity, and to them I clung. I saw Stein again, and again, briefly, he lifted my mood. There had been a development, the only positive news in this bleak period. His doctors discovered that the lesion in his spinal cord was incomplete, which meant he would walk again. Already he was beginning to recover sensation. He could use a wheelchair once they took the body jacket off. He told me his psyche was in better shape than mine but I probably had superior bowel control. A snort of dark laughter from me. I asked him about his wife and he said he had no time for her. He was too busy with himself.

'How so?'

'Recovery takes work,' he said. 'It's a full-time job.'

I wasn't sure whether his wife would understand this. I encountered her in the hospital lobby as I left. She was wearing a sheepskin coat that made her look fiercer than usual, like some lost Hun who'd wandered down from Westchester in error. The weather had turned cool and windy, and her hair was tousled, her eyes streaming. She dabbed at her face with a tissue as she frowned into the mirror of her compact.

'Mrs. Stein,' I said.

The compact snapped shut. 'Dr. Weir. Have you been to see Joe?'

'Yes. The news is good.'

'No thanks to you.'

'What?'

'You know I don't have a very high opinion of psychiatry.'

'Nor of psychiatrists, apparently.'

She'd never declared her hostility so directly, and I was in no mood for it. She stood before me with her hands plunged deep in the fur-lined pockets of her sheepskin coat, this small, angry woman from the suburbs.

'Shall we sit down?'

'I don't have much time. Look, Joe gave plenty of warning that he might try to kill himself, and what good were you?'

'I know what it must look like to you — '

'He was a danger to himself. Why didn't you have him committed?'

'I know how you must feel — '

'Or doped him to the eyeballs so he couldn't think — '

'Will you *listen* to me?'

The entire lobby fell silent. The nurses at reception gazed at me. The security men gazed at me. The scattering of people in the waiting area looked up from their magazines and newspapers and gazed at me. I saw then that not only had I shouted at her, I had lifted my fist.

'Are you going to attack me?' Stein's wife said.

'I'm sorry,' I said, 'but you seem to have an inflated idea of what I can and cannot do. Many of my patients threaten suicide — '

That's when it happened. It was the word *suicide.* I saw Danny sprawled on the floor of his apartment, with a gun on the floor beside him. There was an acrid smell. His blood and brains were splashed across the window. I saw the unspeakable mess he'd made of his skull, the bloody shards of bony matter, the impression of there being only part of a head. His *face:* his eyes were open and he looked startled. I was only dimly aware of the woman's voice. I was deathly cold, shivering, and I couldn't seem to get enough air, I had to get out of there. I walked toward the entrance and heard as though from a great distance my name being called. I emerged onto the street and felt a blast of wind off the East River. Still very badly shaken I limped blindly away from the hospital and found myself some minutes later at the fish market. It was not yet four in the afternoon.

It had never been so vivid before. I'd never been so aware of what it looked like, what it smelled like. That strong, acrid tang in the air, was it cordite? The window was splattered with blood and brain matter that had created trailing globular lines down the glass. And he had looked startled, surprised, *irritated*, this dead man. I was at least relieved that I'd walked away from Stein's wife without losing my temper. I remembered the moment when the fist had come up as though of its own accord, unaided by any human agency, that's how it had felt. I'd had no intention of hitting the woman. I was responsible, yes, and it would be irrational to think otherwise, but I could remember no conscious desire even to threaten her.

★   ★   ★

The last time I saw Stein was in Westchester. He'd been moved closer to his home for physical rehabilitation. He was in a wheel-chair now and learning to walk again. He showed off his new prowess to me.

'One small step for Stein,' he said.

His mental health grew more robust each time I saw him, and mine decayed. I asked him what he thought about the death of the pedestrian now, and he said he didn't think about it much at all.

'No guilt?'

He stared at the floor. We were in his room,

him in his wheelchair and me leaning against the windowsill. His wife wasn't around. He shook his head.

'Not much. It comes back to me sometimes, late at night, but there's not a hell of a lot I can do about it. That sound callous to you?'

'Does it to you?'

'It's how I feel.'

I would never have predicted that the mind could work with such precision: an eye for an eye, a life for a life. I asked him if it had occurred to him too.

'Oh sure,' he said. 'I talk to the dead guy, you know. In my thoughts. I ask him what more I can do, but he says, nothing, you can't do anything more. Get on with your life, he says.'

'Joe, do you ever see him?'

I knew at once that he did. Or had. His hands were gripping the arms of the wheelchair hard. I knew such hallucinations to be symptomatic, and that when he'd finished with his guilt he would no longer see the man whose death he had caused. The same was true of my relationship with Danny, or I hoped it was. Though perhaps I'd never be finished with my guilt, and he'd be with me forever. Perhaps it was him I was meant to grow old with, and not his sister.

'Yeah, I saw him,' said Stein.

'Often?'

'It varied. There were days I'd see him two, three times. Then for weeks, nothing.'

'And the day you tried to kill yourself?'

'He was everywhere.'

I needed no clarification. He was everywhere. There had been times Danny was everywhere. I was better able to cope with this than Stein because I understood the pathology. But Stein hadn't seen the dead man since his fall. It confirmed to me that he was recovering.

I didn't visit him again. There was no need to. But I missed him. He was an uncomplicated man to whom a complicated mischance had occurred. He wasn't to blame for it, but the unconscious doesn't care for such distinctions. The unconscious operates like fate in this regard. Stein's story had an almost mythical shape to it, the offering of his own blood for the blood he had spilled, the subsequent purging of guilt, the atonement. It occurred to me that I might achieve a similar outcome by similar means, the downside being that unlike Stein I probably wouldn't survive the fall.

* * *

But I contemplated it. That night I stood out in the wind on my fire escape, my clothes flapping about me. It was eleven stories down to the street. Vehicles, people, all were very tiny from up here. To the south the twin towers, to the west, where the street opened out to the highway, the emptiness of the night sky over the river. I rattled the railing and heard the rusted rivets creak as they shifted about in their housings. It wasn't difficult to imagine the whole thing coming loose, and me stepping into space.

16

Walt left for Europe with his family. I went up to see them the night before their departure. The children were excited. I'd been to the bank and brought each of them what seemed a huge amount of lira but was actually a small sum of money. I was briefly very popular. Watching them as they finished their packing, hearing the unending stream of questions as to what Italy would be like, what they could bring with them, and Lucia overseeing this scene of mild chaos with placid authority, it was hard not to think of my own family. I knew what happened to children who lived with one parent, how in time they became indifferent to the absent father unless great care was taken. And though I could still see Cassie on the weekends, I had begun to hope for much more than that.

Walt wanted to give me a set of keys so I could sleep in the apartment every so often, to give the appearance that the place was occupied. We were sitting at the kitchen table, beneath the metal ring with the copper-bottomed pots and pans hanging from hooks.

He gazed at me, frowning. 'You depressed?'

He knew how our mother had suffered, and he knew my own history.

'It comes and goes,' I said. 'You know.'

'You have to take care of yourself.'

'Sure.'

'Try again with Nora, will you?'

I didn't say anything.

'Don't break her heart,' he said.

'Walter, what exactly is that supposed to mean?'

'Nothing. Forget it. Take a look at this. One of the kids found it in back of a drawer.'

It was a photograph. Thirty years old at least, a creased print in which I saw my mother, my brother and myself standing outside an old hotel somewhere in the mountains upstate. Our faces were just wedges of light and shadow but there was no mistaking the tension in those two stiffly smiling boys, me about six, Walter three years older. Mom was in dark glasses and a head scarf, and she wasn't even trying to smile. My fingers trembled as I held it. I felt nauseous. What the hell was going on?

'I guess Fred took it,' I said. 'It's the Catskills. Can I have it?'

He was watching me intently.

'Take it,' he said.

* * *

I went up again late the following afternoon. My own apartment now seemed to reek of loneliness, the stark, rank, empty den of a lone wolf. What I wanted was the lingering echo of Walter's children. I wanted the atmosphere I'd breathed the day before as they rushed from room to room, clamoring with insistence that *this* doll must come, this toy, this skirt, this baseball mitt. It was silent now. The housekeeper had not yet been in and the detritus of departure lay everywhere, damp towels, discarded garments, breakfast leftovers. It was as though I'd arrived late for an orgy and everyone had moved on without saying where they were going.

I stood in the doorway of what had once been Mom's bedroom. Walt had replaced her old bed with a low modern thing made of white maple, the duvet hopelessly tangled, the pillows all askew, a pair of abandoned jeans on the floor. I straightened the duvet, put the pillows back and hung up the jeans in the closet. I would sleep here, rather here than in my bleak cell on Twenty-third Street. It occurred to me that I might move Mom's bed back up, restore at least that much of the apartment I grew up in.

That night I wandered from room to room and felt I'd come home again. Traces of my mother were everywhere, for despite Walter's redecoration there was no escaping her, and my image of her was the sad woman in the photo that had so oddly disturbed me. Standing in the bathroom off the master bedroom, which was now all aluminum towel racks and white tiles and mirrors, I was reminded of a morning around the time that photo was taken, when I had gone into her bathroom, thinking she was out, and discovered her naked. She was sitting on the toilet reading the *New York Times*. She wasn't embarrassed, though I sure was. No surprise that a memory like this survives; any boy's experience of the mother's body will leave a footprint on his psyche. This was before Fred left her for another woman and everything went to hell in West Eighty-seventh Street.

Some days later I went down to my own apartment to pick up some clothes. Just as I was leaving, the phone rang. I thought it might be Agnes.

'Charlie, it's Maureen Magill.'

'Maureen.'

'Are you all right?'

'Sure. What's up?'

'It's bad news. Leon died this afternoon.'

★ ★ ★

236

I suppose I should have known. I'd dreamed of his death a dozen times, back when I thought he was the only obstacle separating me from Agnes. Pulmonary fibrosis, poor guy. Scarring of the tissue between the sacs, it happens to firemen. He'd been a candidate for a lung transplant, but infection had taken him off that list. It explained his frequent absences from Fulton Street, and it explained Agnes's reluctance to talk about him and, later, her openness to the possibility of taking me back: the role of husband would shortly become available. But she'd ditched that idea. She was too old for experiments.

I thought at once of Cassie, who'd be greatly distressed and would need all the support we could give her. I called the apartment, and Agnes told me in a weary voice to come whenever I wanted. I arrived in the early afternoon and found them finishing lunch. Maureen was there too, and she certainly looked relieved when I showed up. Agnes and Cass were sitting at the table silently pushing food around their plates. I sat down with them.

'Hi, Daddy.'

'Hi, honey.'

'Charlie, thanks for coming,' said Agnes.

'You want some coffee?' said Maureen, who'd taken over from Agnes in the kitchen.

'No thanks. What I'd like is to have a look at Cassie's room. You want to show me your room, honey?'

She stood up from the table and without a word left the kitchen. Agnes lifted her eyes to mine and offered a wan smile. I followed Cassie to her room.

It was as I remembered it. She wasn't a tidy girl; the floor was strewn with her clothes, the walls covered with posters of pop stars and movie actors. She had a little dressing table littered with cheap costume jewelry, and strips of glittery material hung from her mirror. She'd assembled on her bed the stuffed animals she'd had as a little girl, to remind herself of a time when she'd felt safe.

'I remember this teddy bear,' I said, picking up a very chewed and battered stuffed animal and smoothing its mangy fur.

'His name is Albert,' said Cass.

'I know. He looks pretty sad today. You sad, Albert?'

'Everybody's sad, Daddy,' she said reproachfully, as though I thought Albert was the only one.

'Are you sad, honey?'

She sat on the side of the bed and nodded glumly. I was sitting on the carpet with Albert in my lap. 'I think you loved Leon a lot,' I said.

That did it. She was in my lap, Albert having been tossed aside, her arms around my neck, weeping her little heart out. She told me how kind he was to her, even though she wasn't very nice to him.

'Cassie, he didn't mind,' I said softly. 'He understood. It's not easy, having two daddies. You handled it really well. I was proud of you.'

'No, I *didn't*, Daddy. I was so *mean* to him.' Another squall of tears, her head pressed against my shirt.

'He understood. He was a wise man.'

Then she was out of my lap and opening a drawer in her dresser, from which she produced a number of small treasures, all gifts from Leon. She knelt on the carpet and laid them out, one by one. There was the silver dollar given him by his own father. Beside it she placed the first badge he'd ever worn as a fireman. Then a ring with a huge green stone, and a book of fairy tales. Pride of place went to an autographed photo of Donny Osmond.

'How on earth did he get this?' I asked, gazing with awe at the puppy features of the boy wonder.

'He said he saved him when he was trapped in a burning building. But I think he sent away for it.'

'He might have saved him,' I said.

'Oh, Daddy,' said Cass, 'don't be naive.'

Who taught her that word? I felt a familiar pang; it hadn't been me.

'Will you miss him?'

She sat on the carpet, gazing at me. Then her face crumpled again, and there were more tears. I wanted her to have a very good cry. She must talk about Leon and feel no reluctance to express her grief. After a few seconds she was back in my lap. I stroked her hair.

'But why didn't Mommy tell me he was so sick?'

'She didn't want to frighten you, I guess.'

The question had occurred to me too. Agnes had given me no hint of the seriousness of Leon's condition. 'You mustn't be cross with Mommy,' I said. 'She's missing him as much as you are.'

'No, she's not!'

This came out with a wail. I murmured that it would be all right, and told her again that Agnes felt it as much as she did.

'She doesn't show it!'

'Oh, she does,' I said. 'I saw it as soon as I came into the kitchen.'

She pulled back and frowned at me. 'Did you?'

I told her that of course I did, it was my job

to know what people were feeling. 'We all express our emotions differently,' I said. 'Mommy doesn't cry in front of you because she doesn't want to upset you more than you already are.'

Agnes almost never showed her feelings, and Cassie would understand this one day. But for now it was enough just to defuse her anger. Her mother hadn't prepared her for Leon's death, this was the problem.

We went back to the kitchen. Cassie went straight to Agnes and hugged her. I asked Maureen if I could have some coffee now.

Agnes showed me out a few minutes later. She came into the corridor with me and closed the door behind her. 'Thanks for doing that,' she said. 'I'm not being much use to her right now. I'm in shock, I guess. Thank god for Maureen.'

'She was upset you didn't tell her how sick he was,' I said. 'It took her by surprise. Me too.'

'That was his decision. He didn't want anyone to know.'

'Brave man.'

'I guess so. He's not as complicated as you, or he wasn't, I mean. It was good of you to come.'

She put her arms around me. I heard a muffled sob against my chest, already damp with Cassie's tears. When Maureen first told me that Leon was dead I'd experienced a distinct surge of hope. She pulled back and gazed at me. 'You okay?' she said.

'I still want you back, Agnes.'

I saw her anger blaze briefly. Then it died away, replaced by the tenderness I'd seen a little earlier.

'Nothing's changed, Charlie. I'm sorry.'

'But won't you give us a chance, at least?'

'I don't think it'll work.'

'But you can't be sure of that!'

She turned away. She leaned against the wall. 'I can't deal with you now,' she said.

'Later?'

She shook her head, then went back in and closed the door behind her.

I returned to Eighty-seventh Street. I stood in the doorway of my mother's old bedroom. That morning two men had moved Walt's bed down to the basement and assembled the old bed in its place, an operation I had supervised with close attention. Not a single metal screw, all wooden pegs and dowels: that bed was over a hundred years old. Then came the headboard, and after that the footboard, both carved from black teak and inlaid with panels of walnut. Last, an old chest constructed of lacquered wood that went at the foot of the bed, where it had always stood in my childhood. Walt had spent serious money on this apartment, and there was a sleek, clean, minimalist aesthetic in all the rooms — but one. The master bedroom was now a monument to the past, a shrine to the presence that still imbued it.

★ ★ ★

I slept in my mother's bed that night and was badly disturbed. I grappled through the hours of darkness with intensely frustrating problems of logic, or so it felt, but had a waking memory only of repetitive circular movements of the mind that allowed no resolution or escape, like being trapped inside the mechanism of a clock. Of the specific content of these dreams I had no recall, but I woke in a state of dread. I knew what that meant. Dread signals not the imminence of a catastrophic event, but the presence of repressed memory — the *memory* of a catastrophic event, one that has already happened. But where? In that bedroom? In that *bed?*

That night I medicated myself but it didn't work and I knew why: it was because the mind was overriding the drug. I once treated a man for a sleep disorder and was impressed by the level of disruption it created, how it bled into every aspect of his life, threatening his job, his marriage, his health. It was one of the few occasions in my professional career when I employed hypnosis. I attempted self-hypnosis now, though I had little confidence that it would be effective, and it wasn't, probably because I expected it not to be.

★ ★ ★

The next morning I left the apartment early and walked across the park to my office. I'd been a fool to think Agnes might have changed her mind, and had succeeded only in reopening the wound. I liked to spend all day at the office, even if there was less than a full day's roster of appointments. Once I'd had to turn patients away; that was not the case now. There had been very few referrals in the last several months, not since my mother died, perhaps for good reason. One of the last of the few was Elly, for whom there was little more I could do. She'd told me about the latter stages of her relationship with her father, the period before he shifted his attentions to her sister. The family had an estate in Southampton, and in the yard, whose lawns and trees swept down to the water, her father had built a studio where he kept his fishing rods and his paint box. He was an avid watercolorist. Seascapes, mostly.

Elly invariably spoke in a flat, deadpan tone. The numbing of her psyche in childhood had over the years become a fixed feature of her personality, and it was hard now to imagine her expressing strong emotion, or behaving with spontaneity, or even laughing out loud, though I had no doubt she'd been a normal kid before her father started coming to her bedroom at night. I listened as she talked about becoming invisible so as to escape him. On long, hot summer afternoons he liked to take her down through the yard to his studio.

Later, when she'd gone, I left the office to walk for a while. It was a dank, gray day and there was an uneasy energy in the streets, which seemed busier than usual. People were more hostile, more clumsy, more impatient, more desperate. Was I hoping to avert or undo the terrible event that was trying to break through into consciousness, and whose existence was signaled by this dread? Was it about my mother? All the attention I'd given her, had it stemmed from guilt, then? Had it been not her love but her *forgiveness* I was seeking all those years? Guilt for what?

I felt crowded, claustrophobic, trapped — as though the city was a labyrinth from which I couldn't escape. I became short of breath and began to panic. On a sidewalk somewhere in the East Sixties, just a few steps from Fifth Avenue, I stood leaning on my hands against the wall of a building. Looking down, I saw stashed in a doorway a few sheets of cardboard and newspaper, also a badly soiled quilt and several bulging trash bags. I stood there panting as the crowds jostled me, and contemplated this tragic spectacle. Someone lived in that doorway. Someone would return here and burrow into that stinking heap of cardboard and foul quilt. This was someone's *home*.

★ ★ ★

Leon O'Connor's funeral was held in a Roman Catholic church in Queens, a steep-gabled Gothic Revival building of red sandstone with copious stained glass in its narrow lancet windows. It was raining hard that morning, and I'd left the apartment in some haste and without a coat, but there was an umbrella by the front door and I took it. I was lucky enough to find a cab right away. We got lost twice in Queens and when I arrived the service had already begun.

I took a seat in the back of the church. There were at least seventy people in there, many of the men wearing the dress uniform of the Fire Department. They were all on their feet singing a hymn and their voices boomed and echoed in that gloomy place. The floor was of stone, the pews of dark wood. There was incense burning, and in front of the high altar, close to the rail, the coffin stood on trestles. Agnes was in the front pew, dressed in black and wearing a veil. I couldn't see Cassie because there were too many people in the way. Finally the congregation sat down, and the priest said a few words of greeting. Then there was a prayer. It felt damp in there, with coats steaming and a good deal of coughing and wheezing.

I barely took in what the priest said next. I had eyes only for Agnes, although from where I sat at the back of the church we were separated by those uniformed men, who collectively formed what seemed to me a tribe, one to which I did not belong. I had dreamed of Leon's funeral before, of course, though in my dreams it took place not in a church but at an indoor swimming pool. The unconscious likes to confound death and water.

We rose again to our feet to sing, and I was able to participate this time, for a woman in the pew in front of mine was kind enough to give me an order of service and a hymn book. 'The Lord is my shepherd, I shall not want,' I sang, or bellowed, rather. The last lines were apt: 'And I shall dwell in the House of the Lord forever.' Then we sat down again for the Gospel according to Saint John. As I shivered in the chill of that wet November afternoon I asked myself where my dwelling place should be, for I sure as hell couldn't stay at Eighty-seventh Street. I wasn't able to sleep properly in my mother's bed, and my waking hours were consumed with dread. The idea of returning to Twenty-third Street was just as unthinkable, for it too felt haunted, and most poignant of its ghostly echoes were those associated with the night I'd first gone back there with Agnes. It was hard to forget the brief period of her unpredictable visits, and with them the awakening of a heart grown hard and cynical on the false warmth of prostitutes.

There was a homily and an address. Leon was spoken of in warm terms by his superior officer in his last firehouse. I didn't know he'd served honorably in Vietnam, nor that as a fireman on several occasions he'd performed feats of conspicuous bravery. The point was then made that he'd shown the same courage when facing his last illness, and in this regard

Agnes was mentioned, specifically the happiness and peace of mind she had brought him, she and Cassie both. Then members of the congregation went up to the rail for communion, my ex-wife and daughter among them.

At last I had a chance to see them, though from my pew there was little enough to see. Heads bowed, hands clasped in prayer, they returned from the rail without so much as a glance toward the back of the church. Cassie was in a long black dress with a large ornate brooch pinned to it that my mother had given her, and also Leon's badge. She saw me, but it wasn't until later, when they followed behind the coffin, which was carried on the shoulders of six firemen, that Agnes did. She nodded her head, no more than that, and I nodded back. Cassie gazed at me, clinging to her mother's arm, the tears streaming down her face, and it was hard not to step into the aisle and comfort her, or at least walk beside her, but I couldn't. It was not my place; not my tribe.

Outside the church, in the rain, among the umbrellas, I did speak to Agnes, but she had time only to thank me for coming before she and Cassie were hurried away to the car they were to share with the O'Connors for the trip to the cemetery. There was no special signal, no squeeze of the fingers, no warmth at all. The congregation began to disperse. I felt a hand on my arm and it was Maureen. She asked how I was and she sounded concerned, as if she'd heard I was gravely ill. We were joined by the kindly lady who'd given me an order of service, who now asked if I'd like to join them for a cup of tea, or perhaps something stronger, but I said no. I would have said yes, had I thought I could wait for Agnes as she had once waited for me after a funeral, and history would repeat itself. Instead I went back into the church.

I sat alone in the gloom with the smell of lingering incense as the daylight faded. I had reached some sort of crisis in my life, or a crossroads, at least; anyway, I had to make some decision about my immediate future. For several minutes I contemplated this, then I left. I returned to West Eighty-seventh Street.

★   ★   ★

That night I was in the living room, sitting in the window seat in the dark, as I so often had as a boy, when the phone rang. It was after ten. Again I thought it might be Agnes, and I ran into the hall to pick up.

'Hello?'

'Walt, it's Audrey. You have to get down here.'

Audrey from Sulfur, assuming I was Walter. My brief excitement abated. I could hear the din and clatter of a busy restaurant in the background.

'Why?'

'She's really upset.'

'You mean Nora.'

'She thinks you've already gone.'

She hung up. I stood in the dark hallway. Nora gets upset in Sulfur and it's not me they call but Walter. They call *Walter*. There was a wineglass on the table under the mirror and I picked it up. I wanted to dash it to the floor and see it shatter into a thousand pieces, and why? Because I had nothing and Walt had everything, more than everything, he even took what was mine.

I put the glass back down on the table. I leaned on my hands and stared at my reflection. So it was true. Poor Nora. Had she really believed she could control this exotic triangle, mistress to two brothers, one a shrink and the other an artist? I left the apartment and took a cab downtown. It was a nice conceit, it had flattered her vanity but she couldn't sustain it, not after I'd brought her back to the apartment and persuaded her to tell me the truth. She was not sober, and she'd only just realized that Walter had already left for Italy, and without telling her that his departure was imminent; this was why she was so upset. But it shocked her now to think that he would visit her in my apartment on Twenty-third Street not, as he claimed, because he happened to be in the neighborhood, but because it pleased him to possess his brother's lover in his brother's bed.

He was not the Walter she'd thought he was, I made sure of that. He was not the shaggy pirate of the art world, some latter-day Bacchus with a paintbrush, he was a far more sinister figure altogether, this pathological narcissist who had used her to cause pain to the brother he hated.

After the remorse, the pleas, the tears, the surrender, we went to bed. Mom's bed. We had sex in Mom's bed. Generations had slept in that bed, died in that bed, conceived and given birth in that bed. All that history in a bed. It was Mom's room again, I told her. All it lacked were half a dozen overflowing ashtrays, a few empty liquor glasses smeared with lipstick, a quantity of discarded reading matter and an air of terminal melancholy.

'I can fix that,' she said.

She would have fixed it too, had I let her. There she lay, a pale tiny figure in that vast old bed, with her mascara smudged from crying and her eyes soft and damp. The next morning, as we said goodbye, I remembered thinking that she was again adrift, this woman who survived on a diet of kindness from old friends and lovers and never knew where the next meal was coming from. She was still beautiful, and the damage she'd suffered over the last month or so had only refined that beauty in my eyes. I no longer saw her as neurotic, nor did I believe that her night-mares were the symptoms of trauma; they stemmed, I realized, from the stress of living such a complicated lie, and that was Walter's fault. In fact, I had no need to regard her in terms of pathology at all anymore, but could see her instead as I'd seen her in Sulfur that first evening. I glimpsed it again in my mother's bed, the hint of desolation, the lingering echo of some harrowing hour late in the night when her existence had seemed to offer only dead ends; and if all social life is performance, then Nora's lay in concealing just how bad things must have looked to her at times. She was a brave, doomed soul, and I wanted only to keep her alive in my imagination, as the spirit, perhaps, of some soaring violin sontata —

As I closed the door on her, the decision for which I had been groping in the church suddenly took shape in my mind. I had been looking at the employment ads in one of my professional journals, and a *coincidence* had occurred, if that's what it was. I was far from intact, but I was not so blind as to miss signs, in whatever form they appeared. It had become clear to me that this obsession I had with the idea of home — the pursuit of Agnes, a woman who didn't want me, and this bizarre compulsion to re-create my mother's bedroom, as though trying to return to the womb — it was nothing more than an urge to repeat the past. This is what we mean by *home*, the place where we repeat the past: Freud tells us this, and he also tells us that most of what we call love is our resistance to the prospect of *leaving* home.

17

'Dr. Weir, let us be frank.'

I liked this woman. I opened my hands, the very soul of frankness. We were sitting in my new office. On my desk there was a framed photograph of my mother, and another of Agnes and Cassie. They were my only ties to the past.

'You feel strongly about this,' I said.

'Yes, I do.'

She gazed at me with some displeasure. Tall, big-boned, plainspoken, she wore a dark brown wool suit and her hair was gathered in an untidy bun at the back of her head. Her name was Joan Bachinski. I sat forward in my desk chair and regarded her as though pondering the matter with some gravity. I think she knew there was no gravity. I think she had my measure.

'I had no idea the treatment of this patient would be a source of such contention,' I said. 'I thought I would be easing your burden.'

I was far from home. In a remote valley in the Catskills, a three-hour drive northwest of New York City, near the head of a lake that lies in almost constant shadow, stands a state hospital for the insane known locally as Old Main. It is a Victorian building of granite and timber with rounded turrets and arched windows. To the north and east, heavily wooded mountains march one behind the other as far as the eye can see, and beyond the lake the land rises steeply with no sign of human presence other than a logging road. Old Main can no longer adequately meet the needs of its patients, but there's a haunting splendor to this decaying asylum that I have come to love.

'I encounter a great deal of darkness in my day's work,' said Joan Bachinski, 'as do you, I know. Francis Mead sheds a little light, and I should miss that badly if you were to take him from me.'

'Then he's yours. But you won't begrudge me the veterans, I hope.'

'Have them, and welcome. I'm not much good with battlefield trauma.'

I rose to my feet. We shook hands. The eyes in that weathered face, with its distinct suggestion of underbite in the jaw, were shrewd; it occurred to me that she was probably a very good psychiatrist.

She paused at the door. 'May I ask you a question?' she said.

'Go ahead.'

'Why are you here, Doctor?'

Why indeed? I deflected the question. I told her I was about to ask her the same thing.

'I must look after my father,' she said. 'There is nobody else to do it. But I imagine you are nursing a broken heart. I hope you won't leave us as soon as you feel better.'

An astute woman, and I was reassured by her presence here. I thought we might become friends.

★ ★ ★

I'd seen the Old Main job advertised in the *American Journal of Psychiatry*. They wanted a clinician with my sort of institutional experience, and the interview was little more than a formality. I could have conducted a more rigorous job search and probably done better in terms of status and salary, but I wasn't interested. This was the town where the photo had been taken of Mom with Walt and me in front of that old hotel. The coincidence was uncanny, and I felt that somehow I'd been *intended* for Old Main. This was superstitious thinking, of course, and perhaps the first marker of my breakdown; but it was no less real for that.

Joan Bachinski had shown me around the facility. Together we'd walked the wards, and much of what I saw and heard and even smelled was familiar from my days on the psych unit with Sam Pike. Distant shouts, the rattle of keys, clanging metal doors, footsteps echoing in stairwells and always, in the middle distance, halfway down some long, deserted corridor, a man in loose institutional pants and shirt mopping the floor in slow, sweeping motions; and everywhere that distinctive asylum odor, a pungent compound of disinfectant, tobacco and urine. I was introduced to the ward supervisors, who told me that almost all the patients came from scattered communities in this part of the state, many of them suffering from chronic psychotic illnesses exacerbated by alcoholism. So I wouldn't be challenged, or not professionally, at least.

Every institution like Old Main has among its patients at least one distinctive character, and here it was an elderly man named Francis Mead. Many years ago, before any of his doctors were even born, and while in a state of florid psychosis, Francis had committed murder. I was introduced to him, a thin, white-haired gent of seventy. He washed and mended his own clothes, and in the summer filled his room with wildflowers, he told me. He reminded me of my father; he had the same air of seediness, for it invariably clings to those incarcerated too long. I watched him move among the shuffling schizophrenics and sad-eyed depressives with the sprightly grace of an aging philanthropist visiting a slum, and when he spoke it was in perfect sentences. He was treated by the staff as something of a pet. For several years he'd been in the care of Joan Bachinski, but when I told her, back in my office, that I wanted to add him to my own caseload, she'd objected. I yielded with good grace; I had no wish to antagonize Dr. Bachinski.

Staff accommodation was available in Old Main but I preferred to rent a house in town. I intended to stay awhile, my life in Manhattan having effectively ended the day of Leon O'Connor's funeral. It was an old, narrow, wooden house. The corners were square, the ceilings dry, the floorboards firm and silent after eighty years, and from the front hall the staircase ascended steeply to the bedrooms above, then up a further flight to an attic with a small window from which on moonlit nights I had a clear view of Old Main brooding on its ridge five miles away. It wasn't comfortable, but comfort was no longer what I wanted. Comfort I had abjured.

As for the town, it had seen better days. Once a place of some distinction, its handsome wooden stores and homes were now in a state of disrepair. Paintwork was peeling, rooflines sagging, windows boarded up and everywhere a sense of neglect and decrepitude. I soon found the place in Walt's photo. It was the Western Hotel on Main Street, a large yellow clapboard structure with a broad porch in front and wooden pillars supporting a railed verandah on the second floor. It too was a ruin now, and apparently there were plans to pull it down. I stood on the sidewalk and stared at it, and it stared back at me, sagging, unsafe, condemned, and the blocked windows were like dead eyes, blank and opaque but pregnant, somehow, with secrets, like a trauma built of wood. It aroused a strong sense of dread in me that I couldn't explain.

★　★　★

Several weeks went by. As I'd predicted, the work offered little stimulation, just backward psychiatry for lost souls of no real interest; I was far more preoccupied with my own state of mind. The dread did not let up, it grew worse, if anything, and I began to sink into depression. The first snow fell. The plows were out and the roads were kept passable. I shoveled a path to my front door, not a task I'd ever had to perform in the city. The house was cold at night despite the best efforts of my housekeeper, Magda. She was a weary soul, older than her years, and a good worker, but she couldn't keep the house warm after dark. The kitchen was the most comfortable room. From the back door I looked out onto a field of snow a hundred yards across and several feet deep, a tract of silent whiteness that I found profoundly disquieting. The trees beyond were heavy with snow that fell in loads, crashing through the branches, shattering the eerie quiet of the forest. At night I listened to Rachmaninoff and Elgar, read the life of Nietzsche and the novels of Jane Austen. I often wondered how it would be to tramp off into the mountains and keep going until I was exhausted, then simply sink into the snow and fall asleep. Then the wolves could have me.

To want to die in the forest and be eaten by wolves: another marker of incipient madness. There came a period toward the end of the year when I'd find myself in front of the Western Hotel every day, and given how cold it was, and that nobody spent any more time out of doors than they had to, I know it aroused comment that I stood in my overcoat gazing at a ruin as the snow settled on my bare head. Often the feeling of dread was so strong I'd have to walk away, and I'd go to a bar at the end of Main Street where the road turned up into the mountains. I'd sit at the counter and try to sedate myself. I felt then as I imagined Danny had in those last months in New York.

★ ★ ★

Then came the crisis. I was the doctor on call that night, and driving up the valley I saw through the falling snow that Old Main was ablaze with lights. It was also alive with noise and confusion, for the patients were awake and at their doors, banging and shouting, the staff unable to control them. Francis Mead had for some weeks been suffering a depressive episode that had sufficiently worried Joan Bachinski that she'd moved him to a secure ward. That night he'd torn up his shirt and used it to make a rope. He'd hanged himself from the bars on his window.

I went down to his room with the ward supervisor. Strips of material still hung from the bars. Francis was lying on the bed covered by a sheet. I lifted the edge of the sheet for a second; sick at heart, I turned away. I told the supervisor to get the patients calmed down and move the body off the ward, but even as I did so I heard wheels rattling on the tiles and turned to see an attendant pushing a metal gurney down the corridor toward us.

'Can you look after it?' I said.

'Yes, Doctor.'

'I'll be in my office.'

I went downstairs and sat at my desk, panting. The effort I'd made on the ward had almost undone me; and then that damn *gurney!* I became aware of someone knocking on the door. 'Who is it?'

It was Joan Bachinski. She stared at me for a few seconds, then came in and closed the door behind her. 'What's wrong?' she said.

She pulled a chair close to mine and took my hands in her own strong fingers. They were still shaking. She told me to watch my breath, and after a few minutes I sat back and wiped the sweat from my face with a handkerchief. I straightened my spine. She asked if I'd ever been through something like this before; a suicide, she meant.

'Oh yes.'

⋆   ⋆   ⋆

An hour later she drove me home. I was exhausted. It was still dark but there was a faint gleam off the snow. I decided to take a shower and sleep for an hour, then return and face the day. She'd asked me about Danny, and I'd told her how I'd been the one who found him, how I'd assumed responsibility for his death and how it had destroyed my marriage; and also how my mother once told me that Danny died because I always interfered where I wasn't wanted. Then the nightmares, the flashbacks, the panic attacks, the rage —

'I thought it would be easier up here,' I said.

'How isolated you must feel.'

Her empathy was like balm. For far too long I'd been carrying this burden of ghosts and horror alone. I wanted to weep but I held back the tears; instead I reached across the desk, and once more she took my hands.

'What did you actually think when you found him?'

'I thought, I did this.'

''I did this.' Not, 'I may be indirectly responsible for this.' Not, 'this man was suicidal to begin with, this was always going to happen, anything might have provoked it'?'

'No.'

'And it ended your marriage.'

I nodded. Silence again. I remembered Sam Pike once telling me not to play the martyr, and I remembered too that even Agnes came around in the end to the idea that Danny would have killed himself anyway.

'I think there's more to it,' she said at last. 'What do you mean?'

She was taking some care to formulate her thoughts. 'This shouldn't be as destructive as it seems to be. It's very possible,' she said slowly, 'that the real trauma lies elsewhere. It might be very deep. And I think Danny's just a screen.'

* * *

Three weeks passed, a month, I don't know. More markers of madness became apparent. I saw Joan Bachinski watching me, and her concern for my welfare was palpable. I continued to be obsessed with the Western Hotel. Often I went onto the property at night and kicked around in the snow, looking for I don't know what, I guess my own past, the memory of whatever it was that Joan had glimpsed beneath the nightmare of Danny's death. She was the only one who knew what was happening to me, but at every approach I rebuffed her. Resistance is of course a feature of trauma.

'Charlie,' she said, 'come talk to me, for heaven's sake. You're unraveling before my eyes.'

But I never did. Somehow I got through Christmas, and although Cassie and I talked

265

on the phone she didn't come to see me, which was probably just as well. At times at night I was given to wild elation and at other times there was only a bleak, formless despair. The dissociative states became more frequent, and with them a lingering numbness, a sense of being only barely present in the world. One night I punched out a window in my house and cut up my knuckles. Joan, seeing that I kept my hand concealed, came to my office and got the truth out of me. I realized she was losing patience, and that if *I* didn't do something to arrest this — what? — this *psychic decline* — then she would. She'd do what psychiatrists always do: she'd interfere. This thought alone was enough to remind me of my mother's conviction that without my interference Danny wouldn't have died. 'He'd have done it anyway!' I'd shouted, and Mom had replied: 'No, he wouldn't.'

Then one afternoon I came home from Old Main and saw an unfamiliar car parked outside the house. As I walked up the path Magda opened the front door. It was a cold day with more snow forecast and a few flakes were already drifting down. Pulling a shawl over her shoulders, she ran to intercept me. 'Doctor, there's two men in the house.'

I knew then it was time. It was what I'd

been waiting for, what I'd been afraid of. 'Who are they?' I said.

'They're in the front room. They made a fire.'

I gripped her sleeve. 'Who are they, Magda?'

'One of them says he's your father.'

18

Fred Weir sat in a wing chair pulled up close to the fireplace, holding his hands to the flames. He looked pale and gaunt, cadaverous even, with his face and hands aglow as he leaned into the fire, and when I entered he glanced at me without warmth or recognition. He was wearing a shiny black jacket and faded blue jeans, and there was a black fedora on the floorboards beside him.

On the far side of the fireplace, standing at the window, was Walter. He was all in black: overcoat, jeans, boots. On the low table between them stood an open bottle of Wild Turkey. In my last encounter with Nora Chiara I'd made her see my brother in a very dark light indeed; I'd turned him into a monster, told her that he hated me, that he'd used her so as to hurt me. But to see him in the flesh — to lay eyes, I mean, on the living, breathing man himself — made the paranoia falter. It was Walter, after all. An imperfect man, a flawed man, but no more flawed or imperfect than me. He opened his arms.

I shook my head. I was in no condition for

hearty reconciliations. 'Why didn't you call?' I said.

'Ah, Charlie. You'd have told us not to come.'

'That's right, I would. What do you want, Walter?'

'We have to talk.'

'Why is *he* here?'

Fred seemed not to hear this. He continued trying to coax warmth into his trembling hands and gave the impression he had no part to play in whatever transpired between his sons. It was like having a dog in the room. I went to the sideboard for a glass, pulled up a chair and poured myself a shot of the bourbon. Walter sat down beside me, yawning. He'd flown into JFK only the day before. I'd had little enough sleep myself.

'Heard from Nora?' he said at last.

'Not since I left the city.'

'I saw her last night. She told me where you were. She didn't look too good, Charlie.'

'How so?'

'She was acting a little crazy.'

'That was your fault. You made her crazy.'

He seemed not to hear me. He said there'd been a lot of wild talk and that she'd got drunk fast, a thing she never used to do. He said he knew there'd be tears so he took her home. She'd had a little breakdown in the cab.

'What sort of a little breakdown?'

Now he turned and faced me straight. His tone was funereal. 'You broke her heart, Charlie.'

That Walter should tell me I'd broken Nora's heart struck me as faintly ridiculous. It occurred to me to ask him how, after all his duplicity, all his treachery, he had the nerve to say such a thing. 'You didn't give a damn about her,' I said wearily. 'She was one of your *things*, Walter, and all you needed was someone to look after her. I was your concierge. Your sex concierge.'

'All right, Charlie, calm down.'

Fred was interested now. He'd always enjoyed seeing us fight, and there was a gleam in his old, loser's eyes as I sank back in my chair. Walter had no need to tell me to calm down, I was calm already, calm unto death.

'You remember being up here as a kid?' he said.

'I remember the town.'

'I couldn't imagine why you'd come here otherwise. So how is it?'

I stood up and walked to the window. It was growing dark outside. Something was howling in the forest. All I wanted was to sleep. 'She was in a lot of pain because of you,' I said. 'You never heard her screaming in the night.'

'Oh, fuck off, Charlie.'

I remember smiling when he said this. I returned to the table and refilled my glass. 'What are you doing here, Walter — come to make me crazy too?'

He said nothing. To carry on talking about Nora would only create more conflict, and what was the point?

'Actually,' he said, 'I came because I thought you might kill yourself.'

The answer was so unexpected that I shouted with laughter. Seeing me as a suicide risk, Walter had come to this little town in the middle of nowhere in upstate New York to save me. I stood up and turned on the lamp in the corner.

'You've figured it out, right?' he said.

'Figured what out?'

There was a furtive movement by the fire, Fred flicking me a glance; the dog's ears had pricked up at this turn in the conversation. I saw he was agitated now. He lifted the poker and jabbed at the fire, and a shower of sparks went rushing up the chimney.

'Figured out what the hell happened here. There's a reason you had to come back. You're a shrink, man, it shouldn't be that hard.'

'I don't know what you're talking about.'

Oh, but I did. The building in the photo, that dilapidated hotel. Walter gazed at me, frowning. He got a cigar out of his pocket and toyed with it. Finally he said, 'Remember that dream you used to have?'

'It wasn't a dream,' I said. He meant the dream in which Fred put a gun to my head.

'No.'

He came to the window. We were both drawn there, as if offered some means of escape, some portal through which we could flee the past. The sensation this last exchange aroused in me was hard to describe. I stood beside him and together we stared into the white world outside. It was snowing heavily now. I made a movement of my head to indicate Fred, who was sitting over the fire with his back to us. Walter shook his head.

'Where did it happen?' I said.

'Here.'

'What, this house?'

'This town. On Main Street, that big yellow hotel, the Western.'

A sort of *click* in my head, as of a ball in a socket. The whiskey was biting now. Hardly surprising, since we'd almost emptied the bottle. But I'd at least grasped Walter's confirmation of what I'd already figured out, that my childhood nightmare in fact was true.

It had *happened*. Fred turned around in his chair and glanced from Walter to me, and I think he realized what was going on for he became distinctly shifty.

'So tell me about it,' I said.

'They were fighting. It was a bad one, Charlie. They were making a lot of noise. You went into their room.'

'Ah, shit,' said Fred. He leaned forward and put his head in his hands. He sat there motionless, groaning.

'Where were you?' I said.

'I was in the corridor.'

'Why weren't you with me?'

He stared out the window. Now neither of them could look at me. Later it occurred to me that my brother's cowardice on that long-ago night, in leaving me to do what he should have done, must have been a source of secret shame for years. It was why he hated me. Shame creates hatred. It had done so in my mother too, she hated me out of shame.

'Dad,' I said.

Fred got up out of the chair and now he was like a cornered animal as he moved toward the door.

'Did it happen?'

He gave a sort of sneer.

'For god's sake,' I said, 'be honest for once in your sorry life. Did you put a gun to my

273

head in the Western Hotel?'

'No, I fucking did not!'

I looked at Walter. He was pouring the last of the whiskey into our glasses. 'That's the end of it,' he said. 'You got any more?'

'There's nothing else to drink,' I said. 'So what happened, Walter? Did he or didn't he?'

'No, he didn't.'

'So it *didn't* happen.'

'Oh, it happened,' said Walter, 'only it wasn't Fred.'

'What?'

'It was Mom. It *wasn't Fred.*'

★ ★ ★

Ten minutes later Walter and I were out in the snow, trudging up Main Street to get another bottle. The town was silent. No traffic, no pedestrians, only the falling snow casting a white veil over the buildings on either side of the empty street. The mountains were obliterated by the snowfall; even Old Main was invisible tonight. We felt like the only people left alive in the world. A semi had passed through not long before and left tracks for us to follow. The Western Hotel, a pale hulking ruin in the snowstorm, was as vague as a mirage in a dream. It looked almost benign. We turned at the top of Main Street, by the church, and began climbing the hill. The windows of the trailer homes glowed dimly through the snow. Several were still decorated with Christmas lights. Where the road turned, there was the bar, an old brick building with a neon Budweiser sign in the window. It seemed to promise warmth and good cheer, and we pushed the door open.

The place was almost empty. The pool tables in back were deserted. Four or five men sat on barstools, leaning on the counter, smoking, each one sunk deep in his own wintry thoughts. They turned as we entered, then returned to their silent meditations.

The bartender approached. 'Gentlemen?'

Walt told him what we wanted, and the man put a bottle on the bar. 'What else?'

'Give us a couple of shots,' said Walt.

We'd barely said a word to each other on our way here, but he did tell me he'd had to bribe Fred to come.

'So why did you bring him?' I said.

'I needed backup.'

We sat at a table in that shabby bar and listened to Hank Williams on the jukebox. 'All right, Walter,' I said, 'I'll tell you what I remember, then you tell me where it's wrong.'

'Go on then.'

What a big man he was. I remember thinking this as he put his elbows on the table and leaned in, the bulk of his overcoat black in the bar's gloom, the little tumbler of bourbon gleaming amber between his thick fingers. So I told him what I'd always believed to be a dream. We'd been standing in a dark corridor outside a closed door in a strange, frightening building. Mom and Fred were shouting at each other. Their voices were muffled but we recognized the rage. Then there was the sound of a body falling. All went quiet, then Walt put his hand on the doorknob, grinning at me in the darkness. I felt a sense of rising panic. I knew he mustn't do it but he did, he turned the knob, and pushed the door open. Then he ran away. I was left there by myself. The room in all its horror yawned before me.

'That true so far?'

He flung a glance at me, then lit a cigarette. I watched him as he threw back his whiskey and shuddered. He was staring at the counter where the old men sat. I told him that the next thing I remembered was Fred coming toward me, and the effect was of a giant about to devour me. He had a gun in his hand.

'Walter, I was six years old, and I didn't run away.'

'It wasn't Fred. He was sitting on a chair on the other side of the room. It was Mom.'

'How can you *know* that? You weren't there!'

'I came back. I watched the whole thing through a crack in the door.'

She was very drunk. Her eyes were crazy. Her clothes were loose, falling open; he could see her brassiere, and her hair was wild. She had a cigarette between her teeth. Grinning, she pointed the gun at the boy's head and told him to turn around. He pleaded with her but she just shouted at him to *turn around* and then pushed his face against the wall.

'Give me a cigarette, Walter.'

'You don't smoke.'

'Just give me one. Then what?'

With one hand still squashing the boy's face into the wall she put the gun between the fingers splayed on the back of his head and pushed the barrel against his skull, so hard that he screamed with pain.

'You know what she said then?' said Walter.

I crushed out the cigarette. 'What?'

'She said, *This is what you get for going into other people's bedrooms, Charlie.*'

When she pulled the trigger, nothing happened, just a click. The boy slid down the wall into the mess he'd made in his shorts. It was Fred who stopped it. He told her to leave me alone.

'That's it?'

'Pretty much. You came out of that room on your hands and knees. I took you back to our room and put you in the tub. Nobody talked about it the next day. Mom told me later that if you ever mentioned it, I was supposed to say it was just a bad dream. That's what we did. After a while you believed it.'

'So why did I think it was Fred?'

'I don't know, man. You're the fucking shrink.'

Displacement. Unthinkable, that my mother could do that to me. The unconscious wouldn't sanction it for a moment. So it got displaced onto Fred.

★　★　★

When we left the bar, the snow was still coming down and we were far from steady. The plow had been through, but even so the walk back up Main Street must have taken us an hour. We encountered nobody. Back at the house, Fred was watching for us. He opened the front door as we staggered up the path.

'Where have you two pissheads been?' he shouted.

The next thing I remember we were sitting in the kitchen and Walt was attempting to cook some eggs. I'd drunk myself into sobriety, or so I imagined, but I had no motor coordination and had already dropped a glass that shattered on the floor. I think it was Walter who pushed the fragments into the corner with his boot. An argument erupted at some point, and I remember Walter shouting at Fred to tell me what happened.

'How the fuck do I know?' shouted Fred. He wanted nothing more to do with this excavation of the past. It was just one of the many squalid incidents in his life that he preferred to forget.

'Tell Charlie what you told me earlier.'

'I don't know what you're talking about.'

'Tell him about that night in the Western Hotel.'

Fred tried to light a cigarette but his hands were shaking so violently he couldn't strike the match. Walter stood up and loomed, swaying, over him. I felt a sudden surge of disgust for the old man. He was in an impossible situation but it was entirely of his own making.

'Tell him!'

Something flared to life in old Fred Weir then, as he sat with his whiskey at my kitchen table, a last, flickering impulse of outrage that Walt should be barking orders at him like this. He stood up too. 'Fuck you, Walter!' he shouted, then he was heading for the door, and Walt went after him, but somehow I got myself between them and blocked Walter from hitting the old man, then I was pushing Walter through the back door, my hands on his chest, shouting at him to get the fuck outside.

Then we were out in the yard, our breath cloudy in the cold night air. He swung at me and I took a glancing blow to the nose, which at once started bleeding. With some surprise I watched my blood dripping into the snow. I wiped my face. Walter was panting and snorting like a bull. Then a kind of red flood swept through me and I went for him, and somehow got his coat up over his shoulders, but he rushed me and we floundered around for a while, falling over as we tried to punch each other. A little later the two of us stood coughing, grunting, glaring at each other, neither of us with the strength to go on.

Then we heard laughter. Fred was standing in the back door, framed against the house by the light from the kitchen. He was wearing his black fedora, I remember. He tossed something into the snow between us. It was the black automatic he'd had on Eighty-seventh Street.

'Here it is, boys, you figure it out!'

The childhood nightmare came back to me then, my mother in a dark room at the mercy of this man. The force indomitable, begging him to stop, and me the witness to the sordid travesty their marriage had become. At that moment I hated him more than I'd ever done before. I don't recall picking the gun up out of the snow, but Walter must have guessed my intention because he threw himself on me. As we went down it fired, and it was Walter that got shot, not my father.

Then I was on all fours being sick. I remember gazing down at the mess I was making. Blood, snot, tears and vomit were pooling in the trampled snow, and Walter was staggering toward the house, and I remember screaming at them to leave me alone, to get the fuck out of my house, to just get away from me —

Fred was in a panic, shouting that we had to drive Walter to a hospital, and later I found blood tracked right through the house.

★ ★ ★

They were gone. I was sitting under the window on the kitchen floor. I was thinking about Danny, how he'd been sitting on a floor under a window when I kicked his door down that Sunday morning in the summer of 1972. There'd been spilt whiskey in that room too. Our situations were identical, the booze, the awakened trauma, the gun. I still had the gun. I shifted around until I was in the exact position Danny had been when I found him. I put it between my teeth, then pushed it hard against the roof of my mouth so it hurt, because I wanted to do it right, like Danny.

I sat like that for several minutes. Then I thought of Cassie. I struggled to my feet and from the back door I threw the gun out into the snow. When my mother pulled the trigger that night, how did she know it wasn't loaded? Did she know? Did she care?

I sat through the hours of darkness, shivering in my overcoat in the kitchen. The back door was still open, snow was drifting in, and the room so cold I was chilled to the bone. But how quiet it was up here in the mountains. I thought for a long time about Francis Mead. I felt a strong sense of kinship with the old man. The ward report showed that he'd been asleep twenty minutes before they found him hanging from the window bars. Whether that was true or not nobody would ever know, of course, but I doubted it. That was no impulsive suicide.

The snow stopped falling before dawn as the sky turned dark blue. Hour of the wolf. Only then did it occur to me to phone Joan Bachinski. I woke her up. She listened with close attention as I described what had happened.

'Charlie,' she said, 'stay where you are. I'm coming to get you. I'm taking you in.'

I opened the front door and leaned against the frame. I was all used up. Ghosts were clamoring in my head, I could hear them, I could even *feel* them, they were ripping me apart from the inside. I began to rock back and forth, my face in my hands — and then it changed.

It changed. I lifted my head. I turned to the east. The first light was touching the turrets of Old Main; and when a few minutes later I heard Joan's car in the distance I sank to my knees in the snow and wept. I was going home.

We do hope that you have enjoyed reading this large print book.

Did you know that all of our titles are available for purchase?

We publish a wide range of high quality large print books including:
Romances, Mysteries, Classics
General Fiction
Non Fiction and Westerns

Special interest titles available in large print are:
The Little Oxford Dictionary
Music Book
Song Book
Hymn Book
Service Book

Also available from us courtesy of Oxford University Press:
Young Readers' Dictionary
(large print edition)
Young Readers' Thesaurus
(large print edition)

For further information or a free brochure, please contact us at:
Ulverscroft Large Print Books Ltd.,
The Green, Bradgate Road, Anstey,
Leicester, LE7 7FU, England.
Tel: (00 44) 0116 236 4325
Fax: (00 44) 0116 234 0205

Other titles published by
The House of Ulverscroft:

LET IT BE MORNING

Sayed Kashua

A young journalist, recently married and with a new baby, is seeking a quieter life away from the city and has bought a large house in his parents' hometown, an Arab village in Israel. Nothing is as he remembers: everything is smaller, the people petty and provincial and the villagers divided between sympathy for the Palestinians and dependence on the Israelis. Suddenly and shockingly, the village becomes a pawn in the power struggles of the Middle East. When Israeli tanks surround the village without warning or explanation, everyone inside is cut off from the outside world. As the situation grows increasingly tense, our hero is forced to confront what it means to be human in an inhuman situation.

WINDSONG

Margaret Sutherland

Australia. Martin Ainsworth, a disgraced English teacher, escapes back to his home in the city of Armidale, hoping to recover, with memories of youthful love and ambition. But Annie Marshall, his first love, turns up and the past is anything but dead. Meanwhile, Martin's ex-wife hands over the fulltime care of his teenage son. Confused, Martin turns to Sara, the owner of his apartment, and attempts to steer a course between love and duty. And while Sara and Annie confront their own decisions, the children become innocent participants in the break-ups and regroupings of modern family life and love.

TRUE DECEPTION

Loren Teague

In all the years that Mike McKenna has been a cop, he's never been offered a bribe. That is until Kelly Anderson rides into town on her Triumph Tiger motorbike. She is caught speeding and offers him money. Mike, suspicious about her motives, arrests her. Kelly Anderson isn't what she seems. Her Interpol file says she is a criminal: a drug courier and linked to the Triads. With a shipment of methamphetamine on its way from China, Kelly has strict orders to take control of it. Mike, convinced that Kelly is involved in shady dealings, and against his better judgement, finds himself stepping over the thin, blue line . . .

EMERALD GREEN

Heather Graves

Laura Flanagan leaves Ireland to go to Australia and begin a new life there. During the flight to Australia she meets young horseman Declan Martin, taking the Irish champion Lancelot's Pride to race for the Melbourne Cup. But when Laura tells him she must find an Australian husband in order to live there, Declan doesn't handle it well and in Singapore they part bad friends. However when he walks into the Irish pub where she's working in Melbourne, the attraction is still there. Can Laura recognize true love before it's too late? Will Lancelot's Pride win the Melbourne Cup?